Mel
Enjoy!
xoxo
All the Best!

After the Storm

C.K. Gray

All rights reserved. No part of this book shall be reproduced or transmitted in any form or by any means, electronic, mechanical, magnetic, photographic including photocopying, recording or by any information storage and retrieval system, without prior written permission of the publisher. No patent liability is assumed with respect to the use of the information contained herein. Although every precaution has been taken in the preparation of this book, the publisher and author assume no responsibility for errors or omissions. Neither is any liability assumed for damages resulting from the use of the information contained herein.

Copyright © 2012 by C.K. Gray

ISBN 978-0-7414-7411-7 Paperback
ISBN 978-0-7414-7412-4 eBook

Printed in the United States of America

This is a work of fiction. Names, characters, places, and incidents either are the product of the author's imagination or are used fictitiously. Any resemblance to actual events or locales or persons, living or dead, is entirely coincidental.

Published March 2012

INFINITY PUBLISHING
1094 New DeHaven Street, Suite 100
West Conshohocken, PA 19428-2713
Toll-free (877) BUY BOOK
Local Phone (610) 941-9999
Fax (610) 941-9959
Info@buybooksontheweb.com
www.buybooksontheweb.com

Acknowledgments

I would like to thank my wonderful parents for their direction, assistance, and guidance throughout my life. They have always believed in me, supported my decisions, and stood by my side every step of the way.

I also wish to thank the special man in my life for all his continued support during my journey. I could not be where I am today without him.

I must also include a huge thank you to my three beautiful loving children who have allowed me a life of no regrets. I feel blessed to be called their Mom.

Another thank you goes out to my Physical Therapist. With all his help over the past year, my right hand is well on its way to recovery!

Thanks are also due to my incredibly wonderful friends and fans. If I listed each and every one of you, it would turn into a full chapter! You have motivated and inspired me to follow my dream, continue my path and never give up what I was destined to do.

I could not be where I am today without each and every one of you in my life. Love to all.

~Life is half lived before we really understand what life is all about~

C.K.

Part One

One

Carolina woke up alone.

Too exhausted to open her eyes, she simply lay there, feeling the conflicting sensations of her body. Her skin was warm, almost too much so, from the relentless beating of the sun. Through closed eyelids she sensed its intense glow, a white-hot aura enveloping her limbs and caressing her face.

But then a breeze blew and chilled her to the core. Coldness permeated her flesh, and she shivered, unable to shake it off. Reflexively she brought her arms across her chest, hugging herself to generate some warmth. The problem was she was wet; droplets of water clung to her legs, her face, her bikini. Her hair sprawled around her in a salty, damp halo. Her lips and fingertips felt wrinkled as though she'd been submerged.

She wondered how long she had been there, and where exactly she was.

Bringing a hand up to her forehead to shield her eyes, she flinched at her own touch. Running her fingers tenderly along her brow, she found a welt, a puffy spot she knew had to be the starting of a bruise. Had she hit her head? She couldn't remember. She almost laughed at that—well, how else would a knock on the head affect her? But this wasn't funny. There was no humor in her situation. She was lost.

She was alone. She could barely move. And she couldn't, for the moment, remember exactly what had happened. But she knew it couldn't have been good.

Giving up on blocking the sun from her eyes, she shifted her body a bit, testing it out to see if it, too, was hurt, if she would be able to get up and walk. Beneath her there was wet, scratchy sand; it scraped against her thighs and back, and she let out a low moan. Everything seemed to hurt when she moved, and this abrasion wasn't helping matters any. She gave up on it and stayed right where she was, crossing her arms again to fend off the incoming wind.

She would wait. She didn't know for what, or for whom, but something told her to stay right where she was.

Letting out a deep breath, she tuned out the complaints of her own body and tried to focus instead on what was around her. Somewhere far away she heard a bird calling—shrieking, really, like a seagull as it dipped down to gather up food. One then another—a whole flock must have been coming in. Then, as quickly as they'd arrived, she heard a flurry of feathers, and they were gone.

The only sound then was the beating of the sea.

Hard and fast, the waves pounded upon the shore. Carolina felt the vibration of it, felt their foamy edges licking at her toes. She was near the water. She had been in it. Swimming. Fighting. Drowning.

But how? How had she gotten here? Who had saved her?

Bending her knees slowly, bringing the soles of her feet up onto the sand, she tried to focus on what had just happened.

Just, she thought, but then wondered. She really didn't know. Maybe she'd been there for a while. Maybe whatever happened was far off in the past.

She shook her head slightly, trying to clear her muddled thoughts. She felt a warm trickle of water escape her ear and she shook it again. The sea sounded amplified, the crash of the waves, the pull of the undertow, the hiss of shells as the water dragged them along the sand.

Carolina opened her eyes. Slowly, just a little at first, leaving them at slits for quite a few minutes, letting them adjust to incredible brightness. She was on her back, looking up at the sky. It was bright blue and cloudless, perfectly clear. She remembered lying like this before, not too long ago. Lying on a blanket and talking about—what? Going out on a boat? Yes, that had been how all of it had started.

The sun hung at an angle in the sky, indicating it was late afternoon. Carolina brought her hand back up to her brow and positioned it between her eyes and the sun, then opened them fully. Turning her head to the left, she could see for what seemed like miles down the beach—a plethora of white sand and crystal-blue water rolling over and over in those headstrong waves, but nothing else. Not a person, not a bird, not even a boat. She knew a boat had something to do with this.

She sat up. It took a while—her arms felt numb and would barely support her slim frame. But she managed it. Once upright she tried to reach around to brush the sand off her back as much as she could, but her hands wouldn't reach that far. Slowly she checked over her body for more injuries, finding a few more bruises and nasty welts.

"How did I get those?" she murmured, fingering a red spot on her knee. She wished she could remember something—anything. The name of the boat, why she had been on it, how she'd gotten off it, who she had—

She stopped cold. Automatically her hands went up to her heart, clasping together in front of it. Something in there tugged and ached, reminding her there was something to remember.

Who had she been with? She wasn't alone here. Or, at least, she hadn't been. She closed her eyes again.

"Think, think!" she told herself as she tucked her chin down to her breast, trying to shut out all sensations around her. No more nuclear sun. No more deafening waves. No more screeching sea gulls and no more scratchy sand beneath her legs. Though these minor things had been huge to her a moment earlier, had been all-consuming of her thoughts, they were nothing now because there was something more important she had to think of. Something. Someone.

Someone.

She thought back to the blanket.

They had been lying here, right here on the beach, talking and laughing and enjoying this beautiful day together. Here on this beach. Where they had been for some time. Living. Playing. Making love on this very scratchy sand, beneath this same sky.

She looked up now. She'd seen the stars here. There were so many of them in the inky night sky. Lying on her back, looking over his shoulder as he—

"He," she said. It was coming to her. Something in her brain ignited, like the striking of a match. Just a flicker, a bit of flame to light the way to the memory for which she searched.

She looked out at the water now. She remembered the boat. A small sailboat. Remembered how it rocked in the waves, how eerily silent it was out in the middle of the sea. He had kissed here there, and said he loved her.

"More than anything or anyone," she whispered, his words coming back to her now. That was what he had said.

She had felt so at peace out there, so happy and so very much in love, so loved as she had never been loved before.

The sea was calm now, as it had been when they'd gone out in the boat. But Carolina sensed something had changed. Something had happened in between then and now. She gazed out at the water still, trying to figure out what it was.

And then she saw it. Out on the horizon. A thin line of dark clouds, churning and racing away from her, toward the end of the world. Looked like a massive storm.

She remembered. She'd been right in the middle of it.

"Oh my God!" Carolina yelled as the flashback hit her. Without thinking, she tried to jump to her feet, but her weakened legs wouldn't let her. She sank back down again, half-reclining on her side, one hand scratching absently at the sand, one covering her mouth to stifle her silent scream.

She remembered it all: Falling asleep on the boat. Waking up to the cold, crisp air that foretold of a storm. The boat tossing, throwing her around. The enormous black cloud. The thunder. The lightning.

And then nothingness. She had fallen overboard and been sucked under by the choppy, violent sea. Underwater she couldn't tell right from left, up from down. It was all darkness, all suffocating despair. She had tried to swim, but she was frantic, and the more she struggled, the harder it became to move. Finally she'd just stopped. She'd given up.

She'd thought she'd died.

But then she felt two strong arms around her, and somebody calling her name. She was floating, the rain falling on her face, the lightning striking the water practically right at their sides. But they were together. And he had saved her.

"Michael," she cried, tears now running down her cheeks. She sat up, not thinking about the pain all over her body. It didn't matter anymore. She couldn't feel it. Every part of her being was overtaken by grief.

"Michael," she wailed again, hugging herself once more, rocking herself back and forth as she cried and cried. He had saved her, that much she remembered, but after that, she had no idea what happened. All she knew was she was alone now—she had woken up not with the love of her life beside her but on her own. A castaway, tossed up on the shore by the unfriendly sea, doomed to a solitary existence. Stranded in paradise.

His face came to her. His beautiful eyes, the slight creases around their corners when he laughed, his smile that lit up the entire world. She remembered the feel of running her fingers through his dark-brown hair, across his muscled arms and chest, down his strong legs. She breathed in deeply, remembering his unique and particular scent.

This was the man she loved. Her soul mate. And now he was gone.

"Carolina!" She could even remember what it sounded like when he called her name. She heard it, far off and quiet, but still there in the back of her mind. It was like music when he said it, like he believed it was the most beautiful word in the world.

"Carolina!" She heard it again.

"Michael," she replied, wiping her eyes with the back of her hand. She took in another deep, shuddering breath, then looked out to the water again. So calm. So beautiful. As kind as fate was to bring them together, was it so cruel to steal her love away from her just when she'd found him?

"Carolina!" she heard again, and tears once again welled in her eyes. She looked away from the water, unable to bear it for a second longer. She had to get out of here. She had to run—but she couldn't. She tried standing again, but her legs were still too weak to support her. She dropped back down on the sand, utterly defeated, and just lay there gazing off into the distance.

And then she saw him. A lone figure, running toward her across the beach, heading from the dunes down to the water. He went so fast, almost sprinting, kicking dust up behind him as he covered the distance.

Carolina propped herself up on one elbow, squinting to see who was coming her way. It was a man, that was for sure. Dark hair, strong physique…

And then she heard it again. Her name.

"Carolina!"

It was closer now, and she realized it was this man who had been calling her. He had been calling her. *He.*

"Michael!" she cried, pushing herself up on both arms now. She tried to get up, tried with all her might, but still couldn't do it. She was injured somehow, she didn't know where, and she cursed her body for keeping her from running to him.

"Carolina!" he called back, more frantically now that she had acknowledged him. From her vantage point at the water's edge, Carolina watched him grow larger and larger the closer he got, heard his voice become louder and more resilient. Finally he was mere yards away from her, and then crash landing next to her. He scooped her up in his arms and covered her with kisses.

"It's okay," he told her, his voice rough with emotion, his strong arms once again keeping her steady. "I'm here. And I won't leave you. Help is on the way."

"Michael, Michael," she said, holding on to him tightly. Warmth flooded her body from head to toe, and she sobbed. She couldn't help herself.

Carolina knew she would never be alone again.

Two

The roaring of the jet's engine was so calming. Michael closed his eyes against the bright sun streaming in through the small window next to his seat, thinking vaguely about how the light always seems so much brighter above the clouds. Amidst the temperature-controlled interior of the cabin, he tried to remember what it was like to lie on the beach and feel that beating sun on his face. How many days had they done that? How long had they been there? Two weeks, three, maybe more? They'd been lost in time. Once they'd stepped off the plane on the remote island, he'd forgotten about it. He'd counted only moment by moment, looking only to the future. The past for him—for them—had ceased to exist.

Shifting in his seat, he sighed and opened his eyes. He reached out his hand and his long fingers gently pushed the blind down over the window, blocking out the view, the expanse of clear-blue ocean down below where they flew. Would he ever see such natural beauty again? Would he and Carolina know such perfect peace once more? He hoped so. No, he knew so. He knew because he would make it happen, no matter what.

With his other hand, he reached out and, without looking, caught Carolina's hand. He squeezed it, then looked over at her. In the roomy, first-class recliner next to his, she sat with her head back, her eyes closed. She smiled slightly at his touch and though she couldn't see him, he smiled too.

No need to say anything. Everything they had to tell each other was already said.

As the plane reached its cruising altitude, the "fasten seatbelts" light went off with a muted ding. Michael unhooked his and turned farther toward Carolina. Taking her hand in both of his now, he brought it up to his mouth and kissed it, his lips lingering on her soft, perfumed skin. He closed his eyes too and brought his hands up, still clutching hers. He was so tired, but at the same time incredibly wired.

Looking up again, he examined Carolina's face. Her mouth had relaxed, her lips parted slightly, her eyelids only delicately touching. She slept, but it was light, not the sleep she needed. Neither of them had rested, really, not since—

He closed his eyes again, brought his hands back to his forehead as within his mind a flash illuminated a memory. Lightning, all around him, striking the water and the boat as he tried to wrangle the sail into submission. On the horizon a black cloud raced toward them, dropping sheets of rain and bolts of electricity in its wake.

"Carolina!" he had called. She'd been asleep then too, napping at the back of the boat. And why not? It had been such a peaceful day. Michael had wanted to lie down right beside her, fall into perfect slumber with her far out on the sea. Adrift and silent, out where no one could ever find them.

But then the wind had picked up. And the raindrops had come. And he'd tried in vain to get the boat to shore. And then he'd woken her.

He cleared his throat, choking back his emotions. Fear, anger, frustration—he'd felt all of them from one moment to the next, both during the boating accident and ever since then. Why had he woken her? Maybe if she'd stayed where she was they could have rode it out, and she would have been okay, sheltered in the boat. If she hadn't jumped up so suddenly at his call, if she hadn't scrambled across the boat to help him, maybe she wouldn't have been thrust over the side and into the water. Maybe she wouldn't have had to struggle so hard to survive.

Maybe he wouldn't have found her floating and thought she was dead.

Just the thought of the word raised the hair on his arms. He'd never dared speak it yet, not even when he was alone. But that image...the picture of Carolina bobbing lifelessly in the water, her golden hair cast out around her head, her face buried beneath the choppy water's waves. He would never forget that; he would never get over that first moment of fear and panic.

He'd dove into the water because, at that point, he'd wanted to die too.

Still gripping Carolina's fingers, Michael turned to face front again and opened the blind again on the window. They were still over the water, no land in sight. Just like they had been at the moment the boat had been struck. As he'd reached her in the water, lightning lit up everything around them. In the flashes, he'd turned her over...

And, thank God, she'd been breathing. Michael put a hand up to his mouth now to quiet the sob that threatened to wrench itself from his throat. For as terrified as he'd been when he'd first seen her body, he'd been equally happy to find she was alive. He'd kissed every inch of her face over and over as he'd held on to her, determined to protect her not just then but forever.

I'll never let you go, he'd said. *And if by chance we lose each other, I will always find you again.*

He pulled his hand toward her. It was a promise he would keep.

"Michael," Carolina whispered, and he turned quickly to her, bringing her hand up to his chest and clutching it there.

"Yes, sweetheart," he responded, his voice hushed. With one hand he reached out to her and brushed her hair away from her face, careful not to touch the bandage on her forehead, just above her eye. There was a bruise there and a nasty cut, another reminder of that day. She had little memory of what had happened, only saw it in broad strokes in her mind: Boat. Storm. Drown. She didn't know how she'd gotten that bruise.

But Michael did. He remembered it all, down to the last detail. Including what her head had looked like as it struck the edge of the boat and her body went over.

"Could you please get me some water?" Carolina looked at him and licked her dry lips. She smiled again, but weakly. She tried not to show it, but Michael knew she was run down. After what they had been through—after what *she* had been through—he couldn't blame her. This wasn't just something they could shake off.

"Just as soon as the flight attendant comes around," he told her, then once again bent to kiss her hand. She brought her palm up to his cheek then, and rubbed it along the stubble growing there. He hadn't realized he'd gone unshaven for so long.

"I like the beard," she said, her fingernails scratching his chin.

Michael smiled. The simple act felt foreign to him. For a while there he wasn't sure he would ever smile again. But it felt good; it felt right. To be with Carolina, to be happy with her—even in the direst of circumstances, he knew this was where he belonged. Where they belonged together.

Carolina's chest rose and fell with silent laughter, and she tried not to grimace at the pain it produced. At the hospital—a small place on the small island; Michael's practice was bigger and better equipped, he thought—they had said she probably suffered from a bruised rib or two. Thankfully, nothing had been broken, but bruised ribs hurt enough. She certainly wouldn't be going to the gym for awhile.

Carolina gazed deeply right into Michael's eyes. Just then she had thoughts of her kids, her son and her two daughters. She missed them terribly—had every day that she had been away from them. Though at first she and Michael had vowed not to have any sort of communication with the outside world while they were on the island, they agreed a couple of times to text their children. Carolina wanted to hear their voices so desperately but didn't want them to hear the sadness in her voice. Texting was the only thing she could do.

Michael looked back at her, his gaze just as intent. They'd always had this thing between them, this connection when they looked at one another. It was like magic, hypnosis—he didn't know what to call it. All he knew was that when he looked into her eyes he felt like he *belonged* here, no matter where they were. As long as he was with her, he was doing what he was supposed to.

And since the accident, that feeling had only intensified. Like they'd been through a trial and their bond to one another had only increased.

"I miss them too," he said. He knew what she was thinking. He always did, really. They finished each other's sentences. One brought up a topic another hadn't mentioned yet, though it had been on their mind. Now he knew her mind was only on her children, on the relief she would feel

After the Storm

with them in her arms again. He couldn't wait to see his son, Josh, and his daughter, Emily. The lights of his life. His reason for living.

Well, one reason, he thought as he brought a hand up to caress Carolina's cheek.

"What are we going to tell them?" Carolina asked him, and immediately Michael shook his head.

"Let's not worry about it now. We have a long flight. You're tired. I'm tired too. Let's try to relax and just take things as they come."

She smiled at him again, but tears welled at the bottoms of her eyes. She pulled her hand from his and patted his forearm, absently and repeatedly.

"We're doing the right thing. Right?" she asked, her voice hoarse.

Michael brought his hand to her chin and tilted her head until she looked at him again. They looked into one another's eyes. The connection was palpable. Everything else around them—the other passengers, the flight crew, the window and the sun, the plane itself—disappeared. They were lost in their own time, just the two of them together. How it was meant to be. How it was *always* meant to be—always had been, always would be.

"Yes," he told her, holding her gaze. "Yes, we are." He shifted in his seat and leaned in closer to her. He pressed the side of his face against hers and whispered in her ear, his words for her alone.

"Carolina, we have always been one. Before all this—the trip, the accident, everything—you and I, we were soul mates. Were and are. That hasn't changed. But after all we've been through…"

He laughed lightly again, now letting the emotion he felt inside flow out of him. "I mean, it's obvious now, isn't it?" he asked her. "We're meant to be together, Carolina. Nothing—not even the forces of nature—could tear us apart."

Carolina hugged him, her thin arms wrapping around his broad shoulders and back. Burying her face in his neck, she nodded, as vigorously as her sore muscles would allow. Michael felt the wetness of her tears against his skin.

"Fate put us on that boat, Carolina," he said, holding her tightly once again—as he had in the water, as he had on the beach, as he would for the rest of his life. "And we escaped whatever it had in store for us. Now, it's time for us to make our own."

Three

Home. The place where you're always welcome, your sanctuary, where you're comfortable, where you can be yourself. Being home means being loved, being safe, being surrounded by everyone and everything you treasure most in the world. There's no place like home. There's no place like home. There's no place—

Oh, stop it, Dorothy, Carolina told herself, shutting down the monologue in her mind. From inside the cab she looked up at the house, its cream-colored walls, the flowy, white drapery in each window, the trees and flowers surrounding it. She'd designed it all, down to the last detail. She'd chosen the furnishings, worked with the landscapers, decided on colors. It had taken months, but she had finally created the home she wanted—and the home in which she'd wanted her family to live. This was it. Their place of comfort. That she had created for them.

And now she felt like she didn't belong here herself.

"Are you getting out, lady?" the driver asked her, his rough voice startling her back to the present.

"Uh, oh, yes," she said, opening her purse and withdrawing some cash. Leaning forward, she passed it to him over the seat.

"Thanks," he grunted at her, licking his finger then paging through the bills.

Carolina opened the back door and stepped out of the cab, into the drab sunlight of Seattle. Looking up, she saw clouds—the usual midday sky in the area where she lived. It would probably rain later, too. Nothing like the island, where they'd never seen a drop of rain.

Not until—she thought, but then cut herself short. With a shake of her head she got herself going, closing the car door behind her and stepping up to the curb. Turning back to the cab, she saw the driver had popped the trunk. Carolina sighed, guessing he wasn't going to help her with her luggage.

So, she hauled it out of the trunk herself. One large suitcase, one small carry-on—it wasn't much, but enough to make her struggle. Going up the long steps to the house, she cursed as she dragged the bags behind her, their wheels doing nothing to help. Finally on the porch, she stopped and wiped a hand across her forehead.

Carolina's house sat atop a hill—a mountain, really—and from where she stood afforded her a million-dollar view of the city down below. She watched it for a minute, thinking about all the people running around like ants. To their jobs, to their appointments, to the things they thought were important in their lives. But were they? Work, money, prestige, did any of it matter? Carolina had been away from her business for a month. She was sure when she returned, everything would be the same. Everything would have gone on without her. She'd left it in good hands.

How much did she matter, then? And how much did it matter to her?

She shook her head again, trying to clear out these thoughts. There would be much for her to consider in the coming days, weeks, months. Her life was up in the air at the moment, but soon there would be decisions to make. About her job. About her home. About herself.

For now, though, all she had to do was get in the house. She fished through her purse again until she found her keys, then turned to the door and let herself in.

Before even stepping inside, she paused in the doorway. Closing her eyes, she inhaled deeply, filling herself with the scent of her home: the old wood of the floors, the tang of the dried eucalyptus she kept in a vase in the entryway, the lemon polish that was used on the furniture by her cleaning women, the last lingering remnants of David's morning coffee. *This* was home. Not the things in it but the sensations they produced in her. Nowhere in the world would ever smell the same.

With a sigh, she went through the doorway, dragging her suitcases behind her. She parked them in the foyer, then closed the door gently. The click of the lock echoed throughout the house.

"Hello?" she called as she took her cell phone out of her jacket pocket to check the time. Twelve-forty in the afternoon. Everyone was out. Just as she'd expected.

The phone also showed she had a text message. She read it.

Sitting outside my house. Don't want to go back there.

"Michael," Carolina said, her heart aching for him. She wished she could tell him just to come to her, where he belonged. But she couldn't—not yet.

No one's home here, she replied. *Wish I were still with you. I miss you terribly already.*

The next text came back almost instantaneously. *Miss you too. Always with you.*

Carolina smiled and then slipped her phone back into her pocket. She looked up and around her, at the silent house. She felt like she didn't know the place anymore.

Well, she thought, *time to reacquaint myself.*

Leaving her bags in the hall and dropping her purse on the entryway table, she made her way over to the living room, the clicking of her shoes against the hardwood floor echoing to a deafening degree. She walked past the huge, sectional sofa, brushing her fingertips along its brown, brushed suede, pressing down on one of the plush, oversized pillows. How many hours had she spent lazing there, talking with her husband, watching over her children as they played? Quality family time—so many laughs, so many memories. All of them good. Could she really think about leaving this all behind?

Leaving the living room, Carolina wandered into the study across the hall. An office of sorts, it had a big, antique, cherry-wood desk; full bookshelves lined the walls; a deep-red, Oriental carpet lay across the floor. She and David shared this room, she to take care of her business at home, he to catch up on what he didn't have time for in the office. Workaholics, both of them. Another thing that for her, at least, was going to change.

Down the hall and then into the kitchen, her favorite room in the house. Was she a great cook? No one ever complained. She was alright. She could put out a good spread for a dinner party or whip up something on the spot for her kids when she had time. But that wasn't why she liked this room. It was just so airy, so roomy, so full of light. There were windows all over, the French doors out to the patio and backyard, a skylight that let in the sun's first rays in the morning. She had always felt happy here.

Now, she just wasn't sure what she felt.

Out of habit she wandered over to the phone and checked for voicemail. There were a few—a colleague of David's checking on a meeting time, his sister inviting him and the kids over for dinner, a hang-up that was probably a telemarketer. Nothing for her. As if she no longer existed.

Carolina sighed again and clicked off the phone, not feeling particularly bothered that no one had called for her. She'd informed those closest to her that she'd be out of town on business for an undetermined amount of time. And she'd spent so long away from phones and messages and all that, been so removed from the trappings of her so-called civilized life, none of it mattered anymore. Her sense of what was important had changed. Deadlines and appointments, reminders and questions, none of it meant a thing in the big picture.

But then... Next to the phone hung her kids' activities calendar. She brushed a hand over it, scanning what they had scheduled for the coming week: soccer practice and SAT prep for Patrick, her oldest; school-play rehearsals for sixteen-year-old Lindsay; a sleepover for Alexis, the youngest. Almost every day had something for them to do. And all of it was important to them. So it had to be important to Carolina.

Putting a hand up to her forehead, she turned away. Suddenly she felt woozy, warm and dizzy—probably stress, she thought as she made her way over to sit down. At the island in the middle of the room, she hoisted herself onto a tall stool, then put her arms down on the counter and rested her head on top of them. She closed her eyes and tried to clear her mind.

Don't worry, Michael had told her on the plane. She heard his voice in her head now. *We don't have to figure it all out now. Let's just go home and see where things stand. Eventually, when the time is right, the answer will come to us.*

Was that true? Carolina thought. Was that the best way to go? How could they just walk back into their lives like nothing had happened? How could they be apart? She had so many questions, so much turmoil rattling around in her brain. She felt confused like she never had before. She loved Michael, and she knew she had to be with him. They were soul mates, as he always said, and they were meant to be together.

But she loved her family, too. Even David, though they'd grown so far apart. Maybe it wasn't perfect, but it was her life. Would anything she could build with Michael be as good or better?

Carolina sat up slowly. Placing a hand on the small of her back, she stretched, feeling the tightness in her neck. She was still so sore—a leftover, she guessed, from the boating accident. Michael, not trusting the local doctor she'd seen on their little island, examined her himself many times and never did find anything horribly wrong with her. Some bumps and bruises, a cut here and there, but nothing she wouldn't recover from in time.

So why, she thought, did she still feel so bad? It was like the storm had happened only yesterday. But it had been more than a week since that fateful afternoon.

Standing up, she meandered to the French doors and looked out onto the yard. The dark-purple leaves of her Japanese maple moved slightly in the breeze; a robin hopped around on the lawn, searching for worms. Everything was in place here, was exactly how she had left it. For some reason, that didn't bring her the peace she thought it should.

Turning around, she headed slowly back out to the foyer. She picked up her suitcases once again and hauled them up the stairs and straight into the laundry room. After struggling to unzip the large bag, she picked up its contents by the handful and threw it all right in the washer. She paused. A trickle of sand had escaped from a pocket or the bottom of a bathing suit, the grains skittering all around her on the floor. Suddenly the smell of the sea and the sound of its beating came back to her. At night, when the high tide came in, the waves had crashed like thunder. Carolina's mind flooded with the sensation of Michael's hands on her wet skin, the scratch of the sand on her back.

She clutched her stomach. A sharp pain ran right through it, so fierce it almost took her breath away. Another sign, she thought, that her body needed to rest.

After placing the rest of her clothes in the wash and turning on the machine, she headed to her bedroom. Here too she had to stop, look around, and take everything in. The king-size bed with a down duvet. The silk shades on the lamps on the antique nightstands. The vanity where she sat to do her makeup. The enormous closet full of her business and casual clothes, shoes, and purses of all colors and styles.

It was all hers. Yet she felt nothing for any of it. All she felt was like a stranger in her own home.

Another pang shot through her abdomen. Breathing in deeply, she quickly stripped off the clothes she wore, careful to take her cell phone out of her jacket pocket before tossing it all in the laundry basket. She went into the bathroom and took a lingering shower, the hot water washing over her, relaxing her tired body and mind. Then she wrapped herself in her favorite old bathrobe and climbed into bed.

Under the covers, she snuggled in, drawing her knees up to her chest. She punched her pillow to fluff it up, then lay her head down on it and closed her eyes. She was comfortable; she still felt out of place, but she was warm and cozy. For the time being, that was enough.

On the nightstand, her cell phone buzzed. A text message. Reaching over, she grabbed it and brought it under the thick duvet with her.

The message read: *No one home here either. Going to rest for a while.*

Me too, she replied, then thought for a moment. There was so much she wanted to say to Michael; for all the talking they had done while they were away—all the secrets they had shared, all the promises they had made—it amazed her she had anything left to say. But the problem wasn't a lack of words; it was too much. Carolina felt like she could talk to him forever and never tire of it.

Miss you, babe, she finally typed, then sent the message off. It was simple but exactly what she felt.

Miss you too, more than you can imagine, came his reply. *And I love you, Carolina. More than words can ever say.*

She fell into a dreamless sleep with those words ringing round and round in her mind.

Four

"Get out!"

In the doorway to the mud room, Michael ducked as some sort of projectile headed his way.

"Hey!" he yelled, looking behind him where the thing had hit the wall and landed on the floor, right on top of his biking gear. An orange. Its skin smashed open, its sticky juice leaking into his shoes.

He looked back in the kitchen, where Julie stood by the refrigerator, her eyes practically glowing with rage.

"How dare you!" she screeched at him, then marched across the room and hit him. Actually hit him! Just a little punch on the arm, but Michael was so stunned he couldn't respond.

"Where have you been?" she went on. "Why didn't you tell me you were leaving? What's *wrong* with you?"

Michael just stared at her. He hadn't been expecting a very warm welcome, but this was beyond anything his imagination could have conjured. Julie looked livid, furious, violent.

"I... I..." he began, unable to think of what to say.

She hit him again, in the same spot. It started to sting. "Who were you with?"

Michael sighed now. This he'd been expecting. Though he had left her a note explaining he'd wanted time alone, he knew Julie. That she had automatically thought he was cheating on her was no surprise.

"I wasn't with anyone," he said quietly and calmly, inwardly cringing at his own lie. Despite how Julie treated him, he didn't like lying; it wasn't in his blood. That had been the only hard part of his relationship with Carolina so far—all the sneaking around they'd had to do, all the dishonesty.

But that will be over soon, he told himself now as he put his hands on Julie's shoulders and pushed her away from him. He didn't know how yet, and he didn't know when, but eventually he and Carolina would be together. They had to. They were meant to be. And he just couldn't live like this any longer.

"Bull! Don't tell me you weren't, Michael!" Julie screamed, lunging in for another go at him. He caught her hand this time and held it in his strong grip. He closed his eyes and took a deep breath. He was a strong man, he knew it, but he didn't like using his power for this. Estranged as they were, Julie was still his wife. He had loved her once upon a time. He had no business whatsoever hurting her physically—and no desire to.

"Just calm down," he told her, using the hold he had to walk her over to the table. When her legs hit the side of a chair, she sat and looked up at him. Her eyes threw daggers, but there were no tears there. That didn't surprise Michael, but it did hurt him. It was like the disintegration of their marriage didn't even upset her.

"Now," he said, releasing her hand slowly. She set it on her lap and brought her other one up to join it, folding them like a reprimanded child. She looked away from him, across the room, at nothing, as if looking at him was just too much for her. Michael wondered, for a brief flash, if he should have just stayed away. Maybe it would have been better for everyone.

But no, it wouldn't have. And he couldn't have done it. Despite how things were with his wife—and how they had been for a long time now—he would never just leave her hanging with no explanation. And his children, Josh and Emily, well, there was no way he could ever be far from them. Even if his fate was not with their mother, he would never abandon them.

Michael pulled out a chair and sat down next to Julie. He rested his elbows on his knees and bowed his head, rubbing his hands across his face. He was tired, so tired after everything he'd been through in the last week. The accident, Carolina's recovery, dealing with all those well-meaning but clearly inexperienced doctors on the island... Thank God he could take care of her himself. He'd wrapped her ribs and changed her bandages, given her pain relievers, and held her in his arms. There wasn't much more he could do. Injuries like hers just took time to heal, like so many other things in life.

Take his marriage, for instance. This wasn't the first fight he and Julie had. Or the tenth, or the twentieth, or— Michael had lost track years ago. It seemed like they were always disagreeing about something, and most of the time it was about something he had done—of course, always his fault. At some point in their marriage, it seemed, he had become not good enough for Julie. Everything he did, everything he thought, it was all wrong, and she was more than happy to let him know that at every turn. It drove a wedge between them—a big, dark, hard wedge that only continued to worsen.

Was their marriage worth saving? In the momentary silence, as Julie looked back at him, waiting for him to explain himself, he pondered this. He'd tried before, many times, to make their relationship better. He'd worked less, stayed home more, been more attentive. He'd bought Julie many things—fine jewelry, an expensive car, vacations. None of it had meant a thing to her, it seemed. At least, it hadn't seemed to make her love him any more. Her complaints continued unabated, and maybe even got worse as time went on. Eventually he reverted back to his old ways. He spent all his time at his office and on hospital rounds, going home only to sleep. It seemed better that way. If Julie never saw him, it didn't give her an opportunity to get mad at him.

"I told you," he finally said, trying very hard to keep his voice even, "I needed to be alone. To think things through. Life, *us*, our marriage—which has been a war zone for as long as I can remember."

Julie crossed her arms. "So what did you think about all of it, then? What sort of big revelations did you have when you were off supposedly all by yourself?"

Michael looked at her, looked her right in the eyes. They were cold to him, nowhere near as alive and vibrant as they used to be. He and Julie had known each other for so long; they had met as undergrads and been married before he'd even applied to med school. Maybe they'd been too young, but that's how love is: it makes you do crazy things. Julie had been beautiful on their wedding day. Michael would never forget how she looked when he put the ring on her finger. He wondered now how she had become this woman before him.

"I thought about a lot of things, Julie," he said, looking away from her. He brushed his palm across the table, getting rid of some imaginary crumbs. Could he really tell her why he'd left, and where he'd been? And, more importantly, who he'd been with?

Looking back at her, seeing the venom in her stare, he wanted to, even if only out of spite. "Yes," he wanted to say, "it's true, I was with someone. Her name is Carolina, and I'm in love with her. No, more than that, I'm *enthralled* by her. She's beautiful, and intelligent, and she's kind to me. She never yells or calls me names, and *everything* I do is good enough for her. You treat me like a child, Julie. She treats me like a man. There's no doubt in my mind Carolina and I are meant to be together."

But he couldn't do it. Not just yet. On the plane he and Carolina had agreed only to one thing: they couldn't tell anyone where they had been, or that they'd been together. There was just too much at stake, too much to figure out—their families, their careers, so much for each of them to deal with. Though they both wanted to go to the highest rooftop in the city and shout out their feelings to the world, they had to be rational. And take things slow. They had to do this the right way if it was going to last.

Julie was tapping her foot. Actually tapping her foot. Michael looked down at it and almost laughed at the comedy of it. She was so impatient for an answer, she couldn't contain herself.

"I'm just having a hard time," he told her, still looking downward. If he couldn't tell her the truth, he didn't know what else to say. No words that came from his mouth, he knew, would be good enough.

"Join the club." Julia stood up so fast she nearly knocked her chair over. She stormed over to the still-open refrigerator and slammed it. Hand on her hip, she just stood there with her back to him.

"Julie," he began. He wasn't sure what she wanted him to say. Did she need an apology? Fine. "I'm sorry," he said, though the words sounded feeble even to him. He wasn't sorry, not for a moment of the time he'd spent with Carolina, and he was sure that lack of remorse was obvious to his wife.

She had no response. Not a word, not even a hand gesture. She just kept standing there like a statue, like an unmovable monolith. As usual, Michael did not know what to make of her or what to do. He couldn't make her happy. She wouldn't let him. Was it even worth trying? So, as usual, he gave up the attempt.

Without a word, he turned and headed back into the mud room. Bending down, he picked up the smashed orange and tossed it into the trash can in the corner, then wiped out the insides of his shoes with a rag. Slipping into them, he grabbed his helmet from the bench near the door and strapped it back onto his head.

He looked out the window, down the steep, winding driveway that led to the street. Unable to sleep earlier, he'd gone out for a ride. Ten miles had worked off a lot of frustration.

"Another twenty should do it," he muttered, then grabbed his bike and headed out the door.

Five

"Mrs. Hamilton," Michael said as he came into the exam room, putting on a big smile. He'd been back from his trip with Carolina for almost two weeks and this was the first time he'd seen his favorite patient. "How are you today?"

Sitting on the table, the elderly woman grinned back at him—and, he swore, gave him a bit of a wink. Opening up her chart, he put it down on the counter and looked down at it for a moment, trying to hide his amused laugh.

"I'm just fine, Doctor," she said, her speech slow and brittle. "Just here for my regular checkup. And to get my arthritis medication renewed."

Michael read over her chart quickly to see what his partner, Scott, had treated Mrs. Hamilton for while he was away. "I see you hurt your hand." He turned to her, his face concerned. "How is it now?"

Mrs. Hamilton held out her palm to him, pointer finger aiming upward. "Just slipped while cutting a tomato," she said with a girlish giggle. "That other doctor here bandaged it up for me. Said it was nothing to worry about. He's such a nice man."

Michael went over and examined her finger. "Yes, he is," he agreed absently, checking the bit of scab that remained. "Dr. Butler." He looked up at Mrs. Hamilton and smiled. "Almost as nice as me."

With that, the old woman let out a long laugh, looking away from Michael shyly. He had been treating her for all the years he'd been in private practice and had come to love this lady like his grandmother. She was truly old-fashioned, proper and polite to the bone. But he loved teasing her a little bit now and then, just to put some color in her cheeks.

"So how is your—" he began to ask, but was distracted by a buzzing in the pocket of his white coat. His cell phone. "Excuse me a moment," he said, then reached in to retrieve it.

Turning back to the counter, Michael scanned the incoming text message. *Good morning*, it said, accompanied by a snapshot of Carolina—hair askew, eyes half-closed, sleepy smile on her face. Looked like she'd just woken up and snapped herself in the bathroom mirror. While getting ready for a shower, Michael imagined. She was completely undressed.

Now he felt himself blushing.

"Be right with you, Mrs. Hamilton," he said absently, unable to take his eyes from the phone. He ran his thumb slowly, deliberately over the screen, across the image of Carolina's body. He let his mind remember what it was like to touch her all over, to run his hands over her thighs, her back, her neck. On the island he'd spent hours, even days, like that, just lost in the sensation of her impossibly soft skin. And it was all he'd thought about since they'd come home.

Finally he replied to the message, typing, *Beautiful, beautiful. The most beautiful woman I've ever seen. Can't believe you're mine. Can't wait to hold you in my arms. I need to be with you NOW.*

He sent it quickly, then put the phone back in his pocket, trying hard not to imagine Carolina standing in her bathroom, watching herself in the mirror—her long legs, her graceful arms, her smooth stomach, her—

"Doctor?" Mrs. Hamilton asked.

Michael looked at her. Apparently he'd returned to his patient's side and picked up her hand again. He held it in both of his and massaged it gently. His mind had been so far away—back on that island, back on the beach, under the stars with Carolina—he hadn't even realized what he was doing.

"Oh, uh, yes," he said, then cleared his throat. "Sorry, Mrs. Hamilton. So, your arthritis. I know your left wrist is the worst. Has it been bothering you?"

"Well, yes," she replied, then went into a story about how her pain was interfering with her knitting. Michael listened, trying to look interested, but again was distracted by another buzzing in the pocket of his doctor's coat.

Though he wanted, with every cell in his body, to pick up the phone and see what awaited him, he ignored it. *Best to wait 'til I'm alone*, he thought with a smirk. *Who knows what she might have sent me next?*

* * *

"I can't believe you did that," Michael said into his office phone, his voice a low, intimate purr. In his hand he cradled his cell, displaying that last picture Carolina had sent him. "It's a good thing I didn't open it while I was with my patient."

Carolina laughed, her voice low as well, a throaty, sexy sound that sent Michael's mind reeling. "But you liked it, right?"

"*Liked it* doesn't begin to describe how that made me feel. That was..." He gazed at the picture, touching it as he did the first one, as if it were Carolina herself. He imagined it was—imagined what he would do if she were there with him just then—and felt a fire ignite deep within him. "You're incredibly amazing, you know that?"

He could almost hear her smiling through the phone. "I've heard it once or twice," she replied. Of course she had. He told her so every chance he got. He'd never let her forget it. "So, how are things at home?"

Sighing, Michael closed the picture and set the phone down on his desk, his fire doused by this sudden rain shower. He didn't want to talk about home, didn't want to think about the problems he faced there. He just wanted to think about making love to Carolina, of touching her and making her feel good, of making her as perfectly, completely happy as she made him.

He leaned back in his creaky, old desk chair and spun, stopping when he faced the window. The sky was gray outside; everything looked lifeless. How every day had been since they'd been apart. *Home*, he thought. He guessed he had to talk about it—and do something about it. All those problems wouldn't just go away on their own.

"Everything's the same," he said. "Julie's on my case day and night—when she's speaking to me at all. She's hot and cold, like always. Either screaming at me about something or giving me the cold shoulder." He ran a hand over his face. Just thinking about his wife was wearing him down. "How about you?"

"Well, things are alright," Carolina said, though she sounded unsure. "I mean, I guess they are. Things overall seem pretty…normal."

There was silence for a moment. How different their home lives were, Michael thought—his full of turmoil, Carolina's so calm and composed. There had been no shouting matches for her, nothing thrown at her when she entered the door. Her children didn't hide in their rooms, listening to their parents waging war downstairs.

But that didn't mean her life was perfect. Carolina and David might have looked happy, but Michael knew—because Carolina confided in him, as he always did with her—that deep down they were strangers. When she'd come home, David hadn't demanded to know where she'd been. Hadn't even asked. Most likely because he didn't want to know the truth. He'd simply hugged her when he saw her and said he was happy she'd come back. No discussion. No explanations. No intimacy whatsoever. Just a lot of delusion and covering up.

"Carolina," Michael said, and then he let out a low growl of frustration. His eyes wandered furiously over the city outside his window. All of a sudden he had an urge to get up and run, shout, jump—just get up and do something. All this waiting, all this sneaking around, it was getting to him. No, it *had* gotten to him. He couldn't take it anymore. Not for one more minute.

"Carolina," he said, sitting up straight. "Let's tell them. Let's—"

"Michael," she whispered, her voice sounding urgent. "Michael, we can't. Not yet. That's not how we planned it."

"We have no plan, Carolina!" he practically shouted, his frustration getting the better of him. He stood up then, glancing over at the door to his office, making sure it was closed. That old instinct to keep what they were doing secret, to make sure no one heard him talking to her. He hated it. "I know we said we'd wait, that we have to keep our relationship under wraps until the time is right. But when will the time be right? Honestly, is there ever going to be a right time?"

"I don't know," Carolina replied, and suddenly Michael felt terrible about his outburst. She sounded tired, defeated, worried. He hated to hear it, hated that melancholy note in her voice.

"I'm sorry," he said, speaking gently. He sat down again. "I'm sorry, Carolina. I'm just so in love with you. I hate being away from you. I want to be with you every day. I want your face to be the last thing I see at night and the first thing I see every morning. My sun rises and sets on you. You mean everything to me. I can't live without you."

"Michael," Carolina said, and he felt her voice wrapping around him like a warm blanket. Everything about her was so comforting to him. "You know I feel the same. My life wasn't complete until I met you. I didn't know it, but you were my missing puzzle piece."

"Remember the first night we met?" Michael asked her, his mind wandering back to that evening at the fundraiser. He hadn't wanted to go, but Scott had dragged him. Carolina had approached him at the bar. He picked up his phone now and opened that picture again. He smiled and felt the warmth growing in him again. "I never would have guessed we'd end up here."

Carolina laughed. "I had a feeling," she said. "There was something about you. I was captivated. You took my breath away and that has never changed. It never will."

"I'm glad you approached me," he said. "More than glad. Ecstatic. Elated. Happiest I've ever been in my life."

"Are you really? Are you happy, Michael?"

He spun around again and stared out the window absently. *Am I happy?* he thought. Well, in some ways he was. He had a good career. He was successful. In good health. Had two wonderful children. His marriage…well, that was a down point. But he had Carolina, so nothing else mattered.

"I am," he said firmly. "I am happy." He thought for a moment. "But I'll be happier when we can be open about our relationship—when we can shout it to the world."

Now Carolina sighed. "I know," she said. "I know you will be. I will be too. I just..." She paused for a moment, seeming to gather her thoughts.

"Have you changed your mind about me?" Michael asked, the thought suddenly occurring to him.

"No," Carolina immediately replied, with absolutely no doubt in her voice. "No, Michael, no. I love you. With all of my heart, mind, body, and soul. I can't live without you. I can't, and I won't."

"Then let's get it over with. Let's tell our families and get on with our future, whatever that might happen to be."

There was silence again. Michael didn't like it. He didn't want to push her, didn't want to force her into doing anything she didn't feel ready to do. But couldn't she see how it tortured him, being away from her? They saw each other an hour at a time, a few times a week if they were lucky. They met for coffee. They went for drives. On occasion they could slip away to the Chateau Deneuve, their favorite hotel, and be alone again. Those were the moments Michael held on to, those heady hours spent tangled up in the bed sheets with Carolina, gazing into her eyes and feeling completely at one with her. But it was all so hurried, so rushed. They could barely enjoy each other in the little time they had to spare, and they were always worried someone would find out.

"It has to end, Carolina," Michael said, his voice choked with emotion. "I can't live apart from you for one more day."

Over the phone line, he heard her sniffle and knew she'd started crying. She'd been doing that too much lately—almost constantly, it seemed, since that day on the boat. That had to end too. It hurt Michael more than anything to hear sadness in her voice.

"Michael, I can't." She spoke quietly, her words sounding so small. "I just can't hurt them like that."

Michael closed his eyes. He knew she wasn't ready. And there was nothing he could say or do to convince her. It was going to hurt, whatever happened—it was going to hurt not just their families but themselves. Michael had no set outcome in mind, not divorce or moving out or anything, really. He just wanted to be *open* about things. He wanted to be free to love Carolina the way she deserved, in the light of day, not in secret, not as if they were ashamed. He would never be ashamed of what he felt for her, of what they had together. How could he be? They were meant to be together. It was fate. And it was *right*.

"I love you so much," Carolina said, then she sobbed. "I'm sorry. I just can't do this now."

"Carolina," Michael said softly, his heart melting for her. "Carolina. It's okay. I can wait. For you, I can wait until the end of time. I will wait forever and a day."

He just hoped it wouldn't have to take that long.

Six

Carolina hung up the phone and picked up a towel to dry the tears that coursed down her cheeks. She leaned on the bathroom counter with one hand and stood that way for a while, the towel pressed to her face, until the sobbing subsided. Her chest still rising and falling with dry sobs, she tossed the towel into the sink and pressed her palm against her warm forehead. She wiped back her hair, still damp from the shower.

Once her breathing returned to normal, she opened her eyes again and caught herself in the mirror. She looked at her face, her eyes. She looked tired. Exhausted. The light that used to shine from her, the happy glow everyone always told her she had—it was gone now. At least she couldn't see it. How long ago had it left her? The day she's returned home? Or earlier, on the boat? It seemed like since that fateful day, her life had been full of little else but worry. She still got up in the morning and went to work, cared for her kids, saw Michael when she could, and went to bed with her husband every night. But it was all routine…all but the stolen moments she shared with Michael. That was the only time she felt alive anymore. The only time she felt anything.

She opened a drawer under the sink and pulled out a brush, then began attacking the tangles in her hair. Slowly she worked her way through them, staring at herself absently in the mirror, her mind churning around a million different ideas. Michael wanted to come out with their relationship. He couldn't live without her. Did she feel the same? Of course she did. But she just wasn't sure this was the right time.

If they waited, though, would there ever be a right time? So many unknowns, so much at stake. She'd jumped off cliffs many times before in her life—getting married, having children, starting her own business—but this one was different, so different. Higher, rockier, scarier. She just didn't want to go into it blindly. She had to know she would be safe before she took that leap.

"Mom?"

There was a knock on the bathroom door and her daughter, Lindsay, calling her from outside.

"Just a minute, sweetheart," Carolina said, putting down the brush and reaching for her plush, white bathrobe hanging on a hook on the back of the door. She wrapped it around her and tied the belt loosely, then opened the door.

"Good morning," she said, holding her arms out to her daughter for a hug.

"Morning, Mom," Lindsay said with a smile, then stepped into Carolina's arms.

"All ready for school?" Carolina stepped back, then reached out and ran a hand down Lindsay's hair—straight and blond, just like her own. She saw so much of herself in her oldest daughter. She hoped Lindsay would only inherit her good traits, not her indecision or her tendency to worry until it made her sick.

"Yeah." Lindsay raised her hand and pointed a thumb back over her shoulder. "Alexis is getting her jacket. Patrick's in the car."

Carolina kissed her daughter on the forehead. "Okay, you tell him to drive carefully. Watch his speed, the traffic, and most of all the crossing guards."

Lindsay laughed. "He hates those crossing guards."

"I know, that's why I said it. You make sure he obeys them."

"I will, Mom." Lindsay paused, looking at her mother through squinted eyes. "Are you feeling okay? You look a little out of it."

Carolina smiled at her, bigger and brighter than she had to, trying to overcompensate. She knew she looked haggard. She just didn't want anyone to know why.

"I'm fine, sweetie. Just a little tired. Give me a few cups of coffee and I'll be ready for business."

Lindsay smiled, satisfied with the answer. "Okay, well, take care of yourself, alright?"

Carolina smiled too and again pulled Lindsay in for a quick kiss. What a great daughter she had raised—so caring, so perceptive, so responsible. Lindsay would go far in life. Carolina only hoped she would find happiness as well.

She nodded. "Yes, ma'am. See you tonight, okay?"

"Okay." Lindsay gave her a little wave, then turned around and left. Carolina watched her walk back across the bedroom and into the hallway, where she heard David's voice.

"Is your mother in there?"

Lindsay said she was, then said goodbye to her dad. In a moment David was in the bedroom. He stopped short when he saw Carolina in the bathroom doorway.

"Hey," he said.

Carolina smiled wanly at him. "Hey."

There was a silence—a very awkward one. Just like most of their time together had been since she'd come home. They had talked a little, but mostly David had just been glad she'd returned to him; he hadn't demanded answers or questioned her about where she'd gone. In a way she almost wished that he would—that he would show some sort of emotion about it. Hadn't he missed her? Wasn't he curious at all where she had been and why she'd left so abruptly? Carolina didn't want to fight with him, but his passivity just didn't sit right with her. She felt like she had stepped on him and he had just accepted it.

Be a man, she wanted to tell him. *Get angry. Show me I'm worth fighting for.*

But he never did. David loved her, she didn't doubt that, but he just wasn't the type to take a stand that way. He liked the status quo, liked things to stay as they were. Carolina's trip had thrown off his routine; her coming back had restored order to his life. So, he was fine with it. In his mind, she thought, everything was just back to how it had been.

Then why can't he look at me? she thought now, leaning against the doorframe, waiting for him to speak. David looked all around the room—at the windows, the bed, the dresser, anywhere but at Carolina. She wondered what it would take to get his attention. Yell and scream? Jump up and down? Whip off her robe and do a wild, naked dance?

She closed her eyes again for a moment. This was all so ridiculous. She was complaining he wasn't paying enough attention to her but what kind of attention was she giving him? The situation, she had to admit, was a two-way street. Since her time on the island with Michael, since their relationship had solidified and they'd really become bonded to one another, she just couldn't regard David in the same way. She loved him too, she cared for him, but she knew now that he wasn't the man she was supposed to be with. She'd suspected it before; now she had proof. David just wasn't *the one*. Why had it taken her so long to admit it?

"Going to work?" she asked him, drawing his attention to her at last.

David looked at her for a moment but was unable to keep his gaze from fluttering down to the ground. "Yeah." He straightened his jacket, his tie. "Just wanted to say bye." He cleared his throat. "Bye."

"See you tonight," Carolina said gently, again smiling. She hated that this situation was so hard for him. It was hard on her too, but she knew what was really going on, so she could handle it. He seemed uncomfortable, lost, unsure what to do or where to turn. How to handle her. That made her heart ache just thinking about it.

"Right," David said, giving her a little wave. He still didn't look directly at her. Then he simply turned and left, closing the bedroom door behind him. Carolina listened to the sound of his shoes going down the hardwood floor in the hall. When she could no longer hear him, she went back into the bathroom.

In the mirror now her face was even more drawn. She picked up her brush and continued with her hair, running it through her tresses slowly. Her mind was a million miles away. On the island. On the sun. On the water. On the waves. On Michael. His smile. His laugh. His eyes. His hands. His strong arms around her.

Carolina put down the brush. She looked squarely at her reflection.

"What are you doing here?" she asked herself. "What are you going to do?"

Neither of them had any answer.

Sighing, she opened the drawer and tossed the hairbrush in, but didn't close it. Instead she stared inside, her eyes going glassy. She thought back to that island, to the weeks they had spent there. It was the closest she'd been to carefree since she was a teenager. That was how she felt with Michael—like a young girl again, experiencing everything for the first time. The sky was bluer when she was with him; the food they ate tasted better. She felt she was more beautiful, what she said had more meaning. And of course the passion she felt was more intense. She had never felt anything like the touch of Michael's hand. When they made love it was indescribable, like all the good things in the world wrapped up into one moment shared between them. Time stood still when they were together, like they were the only two people who existed in the universe.

Carolina reached slowly into the drawer. Pushing the hairbrush aside, her thin fingers closed around a plastic stick. She pulled it out of the drawer and held it up in front of her.

Little window. Two blue lines. A plus sign. A positive result.

And now we're three.

Seven

"Dr. Sanford."

Michael looked up from his paperwork and tossed his pen onto the desk. He looked at the phone, from where his receptionist's voice had emanated. He sighed. It had been a very busy day and it was only half over; he'd finally gotten a few minutes to sit in his office, catch up on his charting.

He pressed the intercom button. "Yes, Marissa." He tried not to sound exasperated but couldn't keep the tired edge out of his voice.

The phone clicked on again. "You have a visitor."

Michael thought for a moment. A visitor? In all the years he'd had his own practice, he couldn't remember once being paged for a *visitor*. "You mean a patient? Who is it? Do they have an appointment?"

There was a pause on the other end. Michael picked up his pen and turned back to his papers. Just as he was about to start writing, the intercom buzzed once more.

"She's not a patient," Marissa said. "She said to tell you it's Carolina and it's urgent."

Michael stared at the phone. Carolina? What was she doing there? She'd never been to his office before. It just seemed so risky. Why now, of all times? She'd been so hesitant when they'd talked earlier that morning. He couldn't imagine why she would take such a chance, but it had to be something important.

He hit the intercom button. "I'll be right out."

Michael stood up quickly. He buttoned his doctor's coat with one hand and ran the other through his hair as he strode across the floor. Flinging open his office door, he walked briskly down the hallway, dodging patients, assistants, and Dr. Butler.

"Mike, is everything—"

"Everything's fine," Michael said, holding up a hand, cutting his partner's question off before he asked it.

At the front desk, he saw her standing there, her back to him. It really was Carolina, looking stunning in a gray, high-waisted pencil skirt, an off-white silk blouse, and black patent-leather heels. Her long hair was up in a messy twist. As if sensing his presence, she turned around, flashing her red lips and smoky eyes at him.

As always, she took Michael's breath away. It was all he could do to keep himself from running over and kissing her right there in the waiting room.

"Carolina," he said, nodding his head, trying his best to appear professional.

Carolina threw a glance at Marissa, who watched their exchange from behind her desk. "Dr. Sanford," Carolina said, her demeanor very businesslike.

Michael looked at Marissa also, but not quite as kindly as Carolina had. Marissa got the hint and turned back to her computer screen.

"Come into my office," Michael said, holding his arm out to show Carolina the way. She walked ahead of him down the hall, and he directed her where to go. Once in the office, he closed the door behind them and leaned back on it, taking her in. She looked amazing. Beyond amazing. There just wasn't a word for it.

"What are you doing here?" he asked breathlessly. He wanted to sound stern, maybe even a little cross, but found he couldn't. Not while she stood in front of him looking so absolutely beautiful. He moved toward her and put his arms around her waist, pulling her against him roughly.

"Michael," she said, laughing a little. She put her hands on his shoulders and pushed him back a little so she could look at him. "We have to talk."

Michael leaned in against her protesting arms. He laid his lips on her bare neck. "We have to do more than that." He kissed her again, moving down to her shoulder. He undid a couple of buttons on her blouse, then traced her collarbone with his tongue.

"Michael," Carolina said again, this time her laugh low and deep. It excited him, the sexy, throaty sound of her voice. He pressed his body against hers, moving her back toward his desk.

"You're *so* beautiful," he whispered in her ear as he gently lifted her up and sat her down on the desk. He put his hands between her knees and pried them apart, then pushed up her skirt. He leaned down and brushed his lips against her inner thigh.

Carolina gasped. She grabbed Michael's head with both hands, her fingers threading through his dark hair as his lips moved farther up her leg. Michael grinned. She seemed to be enjoying it. He knew she would. He knew every inch of her body, all of her sweet spots.

But when he slipped his fingers up her skirt and started to explore, she stopped him. She grabbed his wrist and guided his hand gently away. He lifted his head and looked at her quizzically. He saw clouds in her eyes, not the brightness he was used to.

"What's wrong, my love?" he asked her, standing up straight and putting a hand on her cheek.

Carolina looked down at her lap. She picked up his other hand and intertwined her fingers with his.

"Michael, I have to tell you something," she began, her voice low. She sounded so unsure of herself, it made Michael worry. This wasn't like her. The Carolina he knew was so strong-willed. She knew exactly what she wanted and had no trouble going after it. Hearing the doubt in her voice made him scared. This had to be serious.

He moved his hand to her chin and tilted her face upward, forcing her to look at him. "Hey. Hey, what is it? You know you can tell me anything, baby."

Finally Carolina looked him in the eye and they paused there, just gazing at one another. The old, familiar magnetism drew them into each other, took them out of time and place for just a moment. They were all alone, not just in the office but in the world. Just the two of them. Michael wouldn't have it any other way.

"I'm pregnant."

In the space of a second, Michael's expression changed a thousand times: from shock to surprise, from fear to acceptance, from understanding to joy.

"Are you—you are—" He couldn't get a full thought out. He backed up a step and put his hand over his gaping mouth. He just looked at Carolina, looked her up and down. She still just sat on the desk, looking at him calmly, a stoic expression on her face. He wondered why she wasn't jumping up right alongside him.

"Carolina," he said, stepping back to her and grabbing both her hands in his. "I can't believe it. You really are? You're pregnant?"

She nodded. "Took the test this morning." Then she laughed a bit. "Sent you those pictures while I was waiting for the result."

Michael laughed too—in fact, he almost shouted. He couldn't contain himself. He grabbed Carolina's face in both his hands and kissed her passionately. "This is amazing!" he said. He put his arms around her and squeezed her tightly. "Amazing. We're going to have a baby!"

He stepped back again then, just far enough so he could look at her. Carolina, the mother of his child. At no time in his life had he been happier than he was in this moment, he was sure of it. He had the woman he loved, his soul mate, his one true partner in the world. And now they would have a family together. Complications and situations be damned, this was the best thing that had ever happened to him, and he wasn't going to let anything ruin it for them.

Except...Carolina still had that look in her eyes. Something troubled her. "Aren't you happy?" he asked. He gripped her hands again, as if that could make her more excited. "Carolina...aren't you happy we're having a baby?"

She smiled at him, but there was no joy behind it. Michael's heart sank. In his elation, he hadn't stopped to consider: What if Carolina *wasn't* happy? What if she *wasn't* excited? What if...what if she didn't want to have the baby? These thoughts flooded his mind now, rolling over and over like a storm.

"Carolina," he said. "Please say something."

"Michael, I am happy," she said at last. "I'm happy we're together. I'm happy we found each other."

"Are you happy you're pregnant?" Michael cut in. He couldn't help it. He felt himself beginning to panic and he had to hear her say it. Whatever her answer would be, he just had to hear it.

Carolina held up a hand. "Please," she said calmly. "Let me finish. I'm happy I'm with you. I've never been so happy in my life. When I first took the pregnancy test this morning and saw the result, I couldn't believe it—honestly, I didn't want to believe it. With everything else going on...with our relationship, and our families, and..." She looked at him imploringly, as if hoping he could figure out her meaning from this disjointed array of ideas.

The thing was, he could. He knew exactly how she felt. This was a confusing time for both of them. They wanted to be together, but they didn't want to leave their families. Neither of them could ever—or would ever—give up the children they already had. Carolina and Michael knew they were meant for one another, but what about the lives they'd already built on their own? Michael wanted to come clean to his wife. Carolina wanted to wait. Now that she was pregnant, what choice did they have? How long could they possibly put off the inevitable?

"Carolina," he said, once again holding her beautiful face in his hands. He kissed her gently, tenderly. He touched his forehead to hers. "We love each other, right?"

She put a hand up to his face. "More than anything," she whispered, "and anyone in the world."

He kissed her again. "And that means we can get through anything."

Carolina breathed in deeply then exhaled slowly. "I just don't know if I can do this," she said, her voice breaking before she finished the thought. "Michael, I don't know if I can go through with it."

He closed his eyes tightly, fighting back the tears he felt building. There it was—the answer he'd been dreading. He wanted to understand how she felt; he wanted to support her. But he just couldn't believe she felt this way. How could she say such a thing? How could she not want their baby? He prayed he'd heard her wrong, but he knew that he hadn't. Her message was very clear. And in the end, the choice really was up to her. He couldn't force her to continue with the pregnancy. If she didn't want another child, that was how it would be. It would devastate Michael. But he would have to live with it.

The question was, would their relationship survive?

"Carolina, I love you so much," he said for what must have been the millionth time since they'd met. But to get her to listen he would say it a million more. He put a hand on her belly. "And I love our baby, too." Feeling he had nothing to lose, he got down on his knees. He rested his head on her lap. "I want what's best for us. I just wish you would change your mind." He blinked back his tears. "We've created life together. This baby was conceived in love. Please think about what that means."

Once again Carolina put her hands on his head. She bowed down over him. "Michael," she whispered, running her hands through his hair. They sat like that for some time, silently, both lost in their own thoughts. Finally Carolina broke the silence.

"Okay," she said. "Michael, I'll think about it. I promise you I'll think about it."

He looked up at her. His eyes were bloodshot, his cheeks wet. Carolina had never seen him cry like this, and he hoped she never would again. He always wanted to be strong for her; he didn't want to be like this. But the idea of losing their child—and on top of that, possibly losing her—broke him down. Just when he'd felt he had everything, he realized he could lose it all.

For the time being, her promise was enough.

Eight

The house was somewhat dark when Carolina arrived home—just a few lights on in the kids' bedrooms. No one downstairs, no one in the office. David had to be in there somewhere, but where?

She pulled her car into the garage and sat there as the door automatically closed behind her. In the ensuing silence, she gathered her jacket, her purse, her keys, but then she just sat there, staring out the windshield at the back wall.

"Move, Carolina," she told herself, but her body just wouldn't agree. She was hungry again, hungry and tired; she remembered feeling both with her previous pregnancies as well but this time, more often than not, her stomach won out. No doubt about it, she had to eat. Then maybe she could sleep. She took a breath and got out of the car.

Inside, the house was as quiet as it had seemed from the outside. Carolina entered through the kitchen, which was empty, lit only by the recessed lights over the counter. It was peaceful, just the way she wanted it. There was so much going on in her mind, she needed some room for herself—a space to think, to gather her thoughts.

She'd left Michael's office that morning and gone right to her own, where she attempted to concentrate on work. She'd always been able to do that—put her personal life aside and focus on her business—and though in the past she had seen this as almost a bad thing, now she was grateful for it. Juggling her husband, her kids, Michael, their relationship, and now an unexpected pregnancy, her mind was constantly reeling. Her work allowed her to put it all aside for a few hours and simply operate on cruise control.

Or maybe it had been more than a few hours. By the time Carolina had noticed it was dark outside the windows of her corner office, high above downtown Seattle, it was well past her usual quitting time. She'd missed dinner with her kids as well as their phone calls reminding her about it. She'd even missed every one of Michael's many texts. In the last few hours he'd sent a dozen.

I love you, Carolina. I love our baby. Please give us all a chance. Let us be a family.

Are you there, babe? Please let me know you're okay. You're on my mind, as always.

Carolina, please answer me. I'm sorry if I said something wrong. Just don't shut me out. I can't live without you.

Carolina, I'm always here for you. Whatever you choose, I will support your decision.

He seemed just as confused as she was.

Michael, she had finally replied. *I'm so sorry, I didn't check my phone all afternoon. I'm fine. Baby is fine. I just need time to think. Don't give up on me, please. Don't give up on us. Love you, love you, love you.*

The message had been as disjointed as her thoughts, but Michael hadn't minded. He had called her immediately and his voice was as full of love as ever. Carolina had ached at the sound of it. Oh, if they could only run away together again, get away from it all, go live out their lives as they wanted to. She had sat on the leather sofa in her office for the longest time, gazing out at the lights of the cityscape beyond her windows, imagining it. She and Michael. Married. A house of their own, something up in the mountains where the air was fresh and clean. Their beautiful child—and, hopefully, the beautiful children they already had. They could build their extended family and a good life together. In a perfect world, that was how it would be for them—for all of them.

Carolina sighed now and kicked off her heels as she dropped her bag onto the kitchen table. A perfect world. Could there be such a thing? Had anyone ever really found one? She'd thought she had, way back when she'd met David. They'd been young and maybe a little naïve, full of dreams and ambition. Had they ever had much in common? Had they wanted the same things in life? They had both wanted to be successful, to have fulfilling careers. They'd both wanted children. And theirs were blessings; both Carolina and David loved every one of them equally and with all their hearts. But was that enough to keep them going for another twenty years? Thirty years? Fifty? At what point would they have to stop hiding behind their responsibilities to their children and really deal with each other and the problems they faced?

She had no answers. Not for anything. Carolina had always felt so in control of her destiny, so sure of what would happen today, tomorrow, and for the rest of her life. She had it all mapped out—or, at least, so she'd thought. Meeting Michael...well, that had certainly thrown a kink into things. *A good kink*, she thought with a smile playing on her lips. A kink she loved dearly and as frequently as possible. But their relationship complicated matters. She didn't know what exactly to expect anymore, not from anything or anyone, not even from herself. This was all new for her. In some ways she loved it, but it confused her.

Clutching her rumbling belly again, Carolina headed to the refrigerator and opened it up in search of leftovers. On the second shelf she found a dinner plate made for her, no doubt, by her oldest daughter. Lindsay was always thoughtful like that. Carolina took it out and tore off the plastic wrap as she walked over to the island. Roasted chicken and potatoes, stalks of asparagus. She picked one up and ate it cold, then another and another. Reaching for a potato wedge, she sat down on one of the high stools. She popped the potato in her mouth and closed her eyes. Pregnancy just made everything taste so *good*.

When Carolina finished the plate, she was full—and exhausted, to say the least. She'd been up since dawn, and she needed to sleep. On weary feet she plodded over to the table and grabbed her cell phone out of her purse, then proceeded upstairs to her bedroom. In the dark she slipped out of her skirt and blouse and tossed them in the laundry basket.

Turning to the bed, she noticed a figure sitting on the sofa by the window. Carolina gasped and jumped, her heart nearly leaping out of her chest.

"David!" she breathed. "What are you doing? What's going on?"

"Come here," he replied, his voice low. Carolina, her heart still thumping, did as he asked.

"David, what is it?" she asked when she stood before him. His back was to the window, and the moonlight coming in through the sheer curtains left his face in shadow. She couldn't see his expression.

He cleared his throat. Then held out his hand. In his palm was the plastic stick. Carolina's pregnancy test.

She sat down in shock.

The silence that followed felt like the longest moment of Carolina's life. What could she possibly say? How was she supposed to react? Obviously David knew her secret now, but how much of it? Did he know about Michael? Did he know she'd run away with him? If not, how much should she reveal to him? She thought of Michael, of the conversation they'd had about telling their families. But that was only about their relationship, not the baby. The little one hadn't been in the picture yet. Now it was, and that brought everything to a whole different level. Carolina could have dealt with telling David about the affair. But being pregnant? It was more than she knew how to explain.

"Where did you find it?" she asked him, her voice hoarse. It was the only question she was able to utter at the moment.

"On the bathroom counter," he replied, his voice low as well.

Carolina closed her eyes and cursed herself. She'd meant to hide it again, to stick it in the back of her makeup drawer. David never would have found it there. But in her confused state, she just hadn't been thinking. Too worried about how she would break the news to Michael, she'd simply left the house and forgotten all about the damn test stick.

"Carolina," David said now, leaning over toward her. With his shifting position, the moonlight hit him differently, and when Carolina looked at him she could see the wetness of his eyes. He was crying, or had been. And on top of that, he was...smiling. This surprised her. David was *happy*.

Oh, God, she thought. David thought the baby was his!

He moved closer to her and wrapped his arms around her tightly. This confirmed it.

What can I tell him? she thought, her mind racing a mile a minute as he embraced her. She brought her arms up and awkwardly put them around him, an automatic response she couldn't control.

"Carolina, I'm honestly so happy. I love you with all my heart," he whispered to her, his hold growing tighter. "I know we haven't been too close for a while but I think this will—"

"Oh my God. It's not yours, David."

The words jumped out of Carolina's mouth before she had any time to think. Immediately she wished she could take them all back. She felt his whole body tense; his arms stiffened as he pulled himself away. He sat back, his face once again in shadow, but Carolina saw the darkness of his expression. Another silence, this one more deafening than the last.

"What do you mean?" he asked calmly, as if her statement truly did confuse him.

Carolina looked at him, wishing she didn't have to do this. But she had initiated it, so it was up to her to finish it. "It's not your baby, David," she said, trying to sound as gentle about it as she could.

David didn't reply; there was silence. He didn't even look at her. He just sat there, palms on his knees, looking out into the darkened room.

Carolina continued. Suddenly she felt compelled to tell him everything, to get it all out there, as Michael had wanted to. If she wanted a resolution—if she wanted to get on with her life—she couldn't stop now.

"I've been seeing someone," she said quickly, before she could change her mind. "His name is Michael. He's..." She paused to consider her words. She wanted to say Michael was the love of her life, her soul mate, the man she'd never even known she was looking for. But to David, she couldn't say these things. It would break him. And that was the last thing she wanted to do. She hoped that he wasn't broken already.

"He's who I took the trip with. When I went away, I was with him. And I'm... David, I'm very much in love with him."

There. It was out at last. Carolina felt relieved, but then she berated herself for it. She had no right to feel good about this. In an instant she had completely ruined her husband's life. He was off spinning in space now, and she was the one who had sent him there. She felt guilty. She felt awful. She felt sick about it.

But she also felt hopeful. Just a glimmer, and just for a moment. But she was hopeful this was a step in the right direction—for her, for Michael and their baby, even for David himself. He was in a rut too, he just never wanted to admit it. Maybe he just needed a push to get going.

"David," she said, putting a hand on top of his. She curled her fingers around his palm, and after a moment, he closed his hand around hers. He turned his head to her. His face just looked resigned.

"I should have seen it coming," he said, his voice breaking a little. He sniffled and his eyes began to well, but he held his chin up high. "Our marriage really hasn't been solid for years, has it?"

Carolina squeezed his hand. "No," she said. She could have gone on, could have outlined all the problems they'd had one by one. But did they need to rehash it? They both knew their love had died long ago. And they knew they'd done nothing to revive it. Maybe Carolina had been unfaithful, but it had taken both of them to get to this place, to the point where such a thing could even happen. In a sense they were both to blame, and David seemed to know this.

Still, something in him wouldn't let him take it lying down. "How could you do this?" he shouted suddenly, startling Carolina so badly that she jumped. "How could you…"

David let out a noise then, something between a grunt and a growl, a frustrated howl that said everything he couldn't. He put his hands to his head and closed his eyes, then took a very deep breath and let it out slowly. "I'm hurt beyond words, Carolina," he said, his voice measured and slow. "I never pictured my future, our future, without you in it." He laughed a little. "I looked forward to growing old with you. Now I'll have to grow old alone." He looked at her. "I'll never love anyone the way I love you."

Carolina reached out to him, another reflex she couldn't stop herself from obeying. Her husband was hurting, and she wanted to make it better. But she couldn't. Not now. Not when she was the one who'd hurt him.

"I love you too," she said. "Just not the way you deserve to be loved." And she meant that. No matter what was going on—even if she were with Michael, if that dream of hers somehow managed to come true—there would always be a place in her heart for David. She had spent decades as his wife, as a mother to their children. She could never erase the relationship they'd had, and she would never want to. "We're just not right together, David. We have a wonderful family together, and we've made the best lives possible for our children under the circumstances. But we have to admit our marriage just isn't working."

David smiled now, weakly though. He looked defeated. "They're great kids." He reached up to dry his eyes and found the pregnancy test still in his hand. He handed it to Carolina. "Yours will be too."

As she took it from him, she began to cry uncontrollably. How could she not love this man? It just wasn't a possibility. He was good to her; he was pure, he was faithful. He just wasn't her soul mate.

"Does he truly make you happy?" David asked.

Carolina wanted to reply. *More than happy*, she wanted to say. *He makes me feel safe, and content, and desired, and beautiful, and a million other emotions I can't even describe.* But she couldn't say these things to David. They weren't what he wanted to hear. So she simply nodded at him.

"Good," David said. "I can't bear the thought of you with someone else, but if he makes you happy… I just wish I could make you love me the way you love him."

With tears streaming from his eyes, he leaned over and kissed her forehead, then got up and quietly left the room. Carolina heard his footsteps retreating down the hall, then down the stairs, and she sat back, unsure of what to do now. Should she follow him? Try harder to make him understand? She couldn't do that. It was clear he was done listening about it. The damage was done, and nothing Carolina could say or do would change it.

She got up, wiping her tears away, and climbed into bed, holding the pregnancy test and her cell phone. She opened up a new text message. The blank, white screen gaped at her.

David knows, she typed. *He found my pregnancy test, and I told him everything.* She paused and thought for a moment. *You have to tell Julie, Michael. Tell her now.*

The response came in seconds: *Everything happens for a reason, Carolina. We happened for a reason. And he found that test for a reason. Going to tell Julie now—wish me luck. I love you so much, babe. Always remember we're in this together—and we're in it forever.*

Nine

"What do you mean you didn't tell her?"

Michael took a sip of his beer and peered at Carolina across the table, over his mostly uneaten lunch—and hers, which was almost completely devoured. "I mean I didn't tell her," he replied, raising his hands in a shrug. "I told her about you, but that was all she'd let me get out. Then she started throwing things. I had to get out of there before she killed me. I drove around until two in the morning, 'til I was sure she'd be in bed, then went back and slept on the sofa. I'm afraid to go near her. She really wants to hurt me."

Carolina took a bite of her pasta. She was annoyed with Michael, but that nagging pregnancy hunger was getting the best of her again. She wiped her lips with her napkin. "So you said nothing about the pregnancy?"

"I couldn't. Believe me, Carolina, I wanted to. I *want* to. You know I want nothing more than to be out in the open about all of it." He reached across the table and caught her hand in his. "And I *will* tell Julie about our child. Just as soon as I can. Maybe when she's cooled down a little. Whenever that may be."

Carolina looked out the nearby window, at the busy city street beyond. She and Michael had never shared a meal together in a local neighborhood restaurant. She almost felt like ducking and hiding under the table. She wasn't used to it, this being on display for the world to see. And holding hands, no less.

Michael caught her worried expression. He squeezed her hand to get her attention and smiled when she turned to him. "Nice, isn't it?" he asked.

Carolina smiled too. Irritated though she was, she couldn't help it. "Yes. It is. It's strange, but I like it. I could definitely get used to it." She paused, examining Michael's face. He had a new look about him—more relaxed, less stressed out than usual. Maybe he'd only told Julie half the story, but it looked like that had removed some of the burden he always carried. Carolina wished she felt the same. She didn't want him to know it, but her revelation with David last night had done nothing but compound the matter in her mind. Now David knew about Michael, and knew she was pregnant. So, where did that leave her?

"What is it, babe?" Michael asked her, lowering his voice and leaning closer toward her. "What are you thinking about?"

Carolina should have known he'd notice. She couldn't have a thought or an emotion without Michael knowing about it. They were so in tune with one another, so keyed in to each other's body language and psyches. He always knew the moment a bad thought occurred to her as if it were written all over her face.

"I'm thinking about the baby," she told him, looking down at the napkin in her lap. She knew his face would change when she said this, and she just couldn't bear to see his happiness go away. "And what to do about it."

She heard Michael sigh, though she knew he was trying to hide it. He took a drink of his beer again, this time a long, slow pull, and swallowed it. He pushed the food on his plate around with his fork. "You're still not sure," he said, not looking at her either.

Carolina twisted her napkin, gripping it so tightly her knuckles turned white. "No, I'm not." She searched her mind for something more to say, and for the right way to say it. "I want to be, Michael. I want to be sure this is the right thing to do. Having a child is a big step. I just want to make sure we're ready. You know this is going to change our lives completely."

His head snapped up then. "We are ready, Carolina." His eyes were on fire, burning with passion and determination. "We're more than ready. We're so very much in love. We're meant to be together forever and a day. If this isn't the right time for us to have a child, I don't know when would be. Everything happens for a reason, remember? We happened. Conceiving a baby happened."

Carolina reached across the table and touched his face, feeling him soften in her hand. He closed his eyes.

"I'm sorry," he whispered to her. "I just love you beyond words, and I'm so in love with our baby already." He looked at her. "Imagine it, Carolina. A little boy or girl of our own, created in love, the most beautiful child. Don't you want to share that? Can't you see how wonderful it would be?"

She drew back again but linked her ankle around his underneath the table, wanting to keep that contact with him at all times. She'd wanted him for so long, wanted to have him all to herself, and give herself to him completely. Now that time had come, and with it this unexpected blessing. Yes, the baby was a blessing, there was no doubt about that. All children were. Creating life was a sacred act, and one Carolina didn't take lightly. But she just worried...

"Will I be good enough, Michael?" she asked him, her voice breaking. "What if I can't be the mother this child needs me to be?" She thought of her other children, Patrick,

Lindsay, and Alexis. How heartbroken they would be when they learned she was leaving them. Because that was what she would have to do, wasn't it? She would have to move out of their house and in with Michael. They hadn't discussed it yet, but she knew it was inevitable. And she wanted it. She wanted it more than anything. But how could she call herself a good mother if she chose to leave her own children behind?

Michael took her hand again. "You will, my sweetheart." He nodded his head firmly. "No doubt about it. There will never be a better, more loving, more caring, more beautiful mother than you." He turned her hand over and kissed her palm slowly. The touch of his lips on her skin almost brought Carolina to tears.

"I just don't know, Michael," she said.

He looked at her again. On his face were written all the things he felt for her, not just in that moment but always and forever. He loved her. He desired her. He craved her. And above all else, he respected her. And because of that, he could wait until she made her decision.

"Well, I do," he said calmly. "And I'll be right here when you come around."

* * *

"Mom, how do you do this one?"

At the kitchen table, Alexis pointed a pencil at her math homework, drawing Carolina over to look at it. After staring at the paper for some time, reading over the word problem again and again, Carolina simply looked at her daughter.

"I have no idea," she said.

Alexis sighed dramatically. "How did you ever start your own business?" she asked.

Carolina laughed. "I hired accountants to take care of the numbers stuff." She pulled out a chair and sat down next to her daughter, then took the math paper in her hands. "Let me give it another shot."

But before she could read it again, the garage door burst open and in came Patrick, with Lindsay not far behind.

"Dude, you have no idea what you're talking about!" Patrick whirled into the room like a hurricane, shouting over his shoulder at his sister.

"I'm not a *dude*, dude," Lindsay shot back, following him over to the island, where they both dropped their backpacks. Patrick headed straight for the refrigerator while Lindsay grabbed a banana out of the nearby fruit bowl and jumped up onto a chair. "And I do know that I'm talking about. You've got these *girls* hanging all over you, and you don't want to leave. I get it. But I don't like getting home an hour late from school every day. You're supposed to give me a ride, not make me wait while you tend to your sad little social life."

Grabbing a bottle of water out of the fridge, Patrick laughed. "Then take the bus, dude," he said. He took a swig of water and tossed the bottle's cap across the room into the sink, throwing his arm up in the air as if he were making a jump shot.

Lindsay just stared at him. "I'm not a—"

"*Dude*," Patrick said, with a mischievous laugh. Baiting his sister was one of his favorite pastimes. He seemed about to go on, but then looking across the room, he seemed to notice Carolina for the first time. "Oh, hey, Mom."

"Hey," she replied, smiling and giving him a little wave, as ever amused by the back and forth between her two oldest children. Patrick and Lindsay had always been competitive with one another, even as small children, and as they grew that developed into a tendency toward bickering and banter. Sometimes they sounded like they were arguing, but Carolina knew it was all in fun. They just enjoyed sparring with one another and loved each other, underneath it all, an incredible amount.

"How was school?" Carolina asked. "Any homework?"

Lindsay got up from her chair and threw out her banana peel, then grabbed her backpack and headed over to the table. "I have a history test tomorrow," she said, pulling out a big, thick textbook.

"Patrick?" Carolina asked, turning back to him. He reluctantly took up his book bag as well and shuffled over to sit down with the rest of them.

"Just the usual," he replied, slowly unzipping his bag and pulling out books. "English essay, Spanish test…"

Carolina sat back in her chair and let her three children take over, chattering with one another as they set to work. Lindsay talked about her plans for the weekend as she flipped through her book, looking for the right chapter, and Patrick helped Alexis with her math homework—*Thank goodness*, Carolina thought. She was off the hook for that. Before long all three of them had settled into a comfortable silence, lost in their assignments and thoughts. Carolina smiled, enjoying this routine family moment as if it were the biggest event in the world. She wouldn't give up times like this for the world.

And with that thought, her mind darkened. Because wasn't that what she was planning to do? Give all this up? If she and Michael lived together, there would be no more afternoon homework sessions with her three wonderful children. There would be no more family meetings in the kitchen. No more evening meals together, no more brunches on the weekend. All the comfort she found with her family here would be gone, erased as if it had never existed.

Carolina put a hand on her chest and closed her eyes. *But it will all still exist in my heart*, she thought. *I have to remember that.* Just because she was moving on to a new phase of her life didn't mean the old one ceased to exist. She loved her children so, so much; she couldn't imagine not having them around. Maybe their relationships would become different, and maybe the time they spent together would change—new places, new settings, new arrangements. But the core of it all, the fact that she was their mother, their protector, the one who had given them life and seen them through it thus far...well, that would always remain. Carolina would always be there for them, in good times and bad, just as she always had been. She would make sure of it. She just hoped they would still want her in their lives.

Carolina felt a pang in her stomach and she opened her eyes. Unconsciously her hand moved down to her belly and rubbed it, as if comforting the tiny, living thing inside it. She looked again at her children as they once again joked and laughed with one another, Patrick throwing crumpled-up paper at the girls, Alexis shrieking, Lindsay batting the paper away with her notebook. And so clearly, for a moment, Carolina saw herself in each of them: in Lindsay's long, blond hair; in Patrick's sparkling, green eyes; in Alexis's quick, ebullient smile. She turned her face away, hiding the tears she knew were about to spring forth. The love she felt for these children—*her* children, *her* family, these little pieces of her—was almost more than she could hold within her heart.

Again her belly twinged. As if trying to tell her something. Carolina rubbed it again, a thought unfolding in her mind.

She got up and grabbed her cell phone.

I can't do it, she typed quickly. *I can't give up our baby, Michael. It's a part of me, a part of us. I want our child. I want it all, Michael.*

And before she could change her mind, she hit "send," then went back to join her children, the weight that had been on her shoulders completely gone.

Ten

Michael knew he was a good man. He'd worked his entire life to become who he was today. From the time he was a young child his parents had always instilled good values in him, taught him to know right from wrong, and gave him strong morals that carried through to this day. In work, in home, in life, he always looked out for his fellow man, protected those he loved, and fought fiercely for what he believed in, even when it did not benefit him—just because it was the right thing to do.

This was all part of why he had become a doctor. Not just because he'd wanted the admiration or the wealth, but because he had a great desire to help people. He wanted to use his strength, his intelligence, his skills and abilities to make other people's lives better. Maybe he wasn't changing things on the grand scale, but in his own little corner of the world, he believed he made a difference. That, as his parents had taught him, is what a good person does.

So why, just then, did he feel like the worst person on earth?

"How *could* you?" Julie slammed her hand down on the dresser, causing everything on top of it to shake: her hairbrush, Michael's cologne, her jewelry box. Somewhere in there were all the precious gifts he'd given her over the years, the necklaces and rings and bracelets, the shiny things she'd worn with such pride. What had they meant to her? Michael had seen them as symbols of their love, as tangible objects to remind her of just how he felt for her. Maybe she hadn't, though. Maybe to her they were just diamonds and pearls, just strings of stones she could use to make other wives envious. Michael had given her a good life; she'd wanted for nothing in their time together. Now he saw these material things simply weren't enough.

Sitting on the bed, Michael cringed. At least she wasn't throwing things at him.

"Michael, how could you?" Julie repeated, her voice halfway between a shriek and a growl.

Michael was glad the kids weren't home to hear it. This was the angriest he had ever seen her. "Julie, I—"

"What's her name, Michael? What's this woman's name?"

When he'd told her about Carolina the previous evening, Julie hadn't wanted to know a thing about her. Too angry and too eager to hurl insults at him, she hadn't asked a thing about her. Julie was all about blaming him, always had been; all she had to know was that he'd cheated on her and everything blew up. Their fighting, their problems. Their years of unhappiness. Suddenly it was all because of what he'd done—not because the love had disappeared from their relationship long ago. Their marriage was like a soaked match; there was little chance it would ever spark again. Why even try? They'd both wondered this deep inside. They'd both given up. But Michael was always the bad guy no matter what the circumstance, never the good guy he thought himself to be. And Julie would never pass up an opportunity to tell him so.

He sighed. "Carolina," he said quietly. It felt so strange to say her name like that, here, in his house, under these circumstances. But the sound of it, just uttering it, brought a sense of peace to him. He thought of Carolina's face, about how soft her hair was. He heard her laugh, smelled her intoxicating perfume. "Carolina," he repeated, more for himself than for Julie, and he tried not to let himself smile.

"I heard you the first time," Julie answered, opening a drawer and slamming it shut again, apparently just for effect. She began to pace. "Well, I hope this Carolina woman makes you happy, Michael, because she and this baby of yours are the only people you'll have left in the world. I'm warning you now, if you leave me, you are finished, Michael. The end. *Finished.* Do you hear me? That will be the end of your life as you know it. No more beautiful house, no more fancy car, no more big, important doctor. I will take everything you have. I will *ruin* you. Ruin you, Michael!"

"Julie, listen." He held up a hand to her, as if that might make her stop. No such luck, though.

"And what about your children, Michael?" she went on, walking around the room and picking up her things—her shoes, her cell phone, her purse. "What about the children you already have? What are you going to tell them?"

Michael felt tears spring to his eyes and was surprised the same wasn't happening to Julie. She didn't seem the least bit upset. She wasn't sad he had cheated on her. Rage had become her only emotion, blocking out everything else.

"Julie, I'll talk to the children. This won't change things between us. I still love them, always have, always will—"

"Won't change things?" She laughed, a bitter, guttural noise that caught in her throat and sent a chill down Michael's back. "Are you serious? You think your running off to be with another woman and the baby you fathered with her *while you were still married to me* won't affect them? They're not stupid, Michael. They're practically adults. They'll see what's going on here. And I guarantee you, they won't be taking your side."

Michael put a hand up to his temple and rubbed it. He felt a headache coming on. This was going pretty much exactly as he'd thought it would, but still it was difficult to swallow.

"I guess I can't tell you anything then," he said. "Nothing you'd want to hear."

"You said it all, Michael." Julie's voice was a hiss now. She leaned in toward him menacingly. "You've said everything you need to. I don't want to hear your excuses. I don't want to hear how much you're in love. Blah, blah, blah, that's all I hear." Her tone was mean now, condescending and rude. "And I have nothing to say to you other than you disgust me. I hate you, Michael. And I want you out of this house tonight."

Belongings in hand, Julie stormed out of the room, slamming the door behind her. There was no need for that. She could have left quietly. But no, that wasn't like her—not anymore. He wondered where the sweet, loving woman he'd married had run away to but knew, deep down, she was never coming back.

Probably for the best, Michael thought, relieved a little that the argument was over. Julie was in the right here, he admitted that both to her and to himself. He had cheated, no question, and that was wrong. He had no defense for it. Under normal circumstances he would have felt enormous remorse for it. But things weren't normal here, and they hadn't been for a very long time. Julie couldn't deny that. They were barely even married anymore, just two strangers who shared a house and occasionally spoke to one another. She said she hated him, and Michael didn't doubt it. That much had been clear to him for a while.

Trying to relax, he lay back on the bed and closed his eyes. *I want you out of this house tonight.* Julie's voice replayed in his mind. He hadn't been surprised when she'd said it; in fact he'd expected it. He would have done the same thing in her shoes. Still, it stung a little. She was forcing him out of his home and pushing him away from his family. Maybe he deserved it, but that didn't mean he had to like it.

If I could just get a few hours alone with Josh and Emily, he thought. He knew he could get them to understand what he'd done. His relationship with them was different; he was their father but their friend, too, and they were always open to what he had to say. Julie didn't have that. She was the authority in the house, the disciplinarian. Michael felt sick about how things would be around there after he was gone. He had to leave; he had to start his life with Carolina and their child. But would this happiness be worth putting his children through agony?

He rolled over and buried his face in his pillow, struggling not to let the guilt overtake him. How could he do it? How could he leave his kids? He rolled over again and stared up at the ceiling.

"They'll understand," he told himself aloud, as if trying to convince himself. His cell phone buzzed and he pulled it out of his pants pocket. There was an incoming text message.

Michael, I'm so worried about you. It was from Carolina. *I wish I could be there. I can just imagine what you must be dealing with. Remember, we'll get through this together. I love you, babe.*

Michael smiled, picturing Carolina right there with him. Lying in bed, holding him tightly in her arms, telling him everything would be alright.

It's done, he wrote back. *Julie knows everything. You, the baby—I told her all of it. All the cards are on the table.*

He took a long, deep breath. He couldn't believe it—the truth was finally told. A mix of emotions ran through him: relief and sadness, confusion and joy. He and Carolina no longer had to hide their relationship. He could love her just as he wanted to, could show her affection wherever and however he pleased. There'd be a lot of explaining to do to the other people in their lives, but from now on they wouldn't have to worry about being seen together. Most important, they could live under the same roof and raise their child in a peaceful environment. Their new life would be far from simple in the beginning but full of happiness in the end.

He sent the message to Carolina, then jumped up out of the bed. He felt like a new man—and definitely one with a mission. Clapping his hands together, he headed to the closet. It was time to pack.

Eleven

Carolina pulled back the sheets on the bed in the guest room. It had been a while since anyone had stayed there, and she wouldn't have thought she would be next. But since she'd told David about Michael and the baby, she just hadn't felt right about sharing a bed with him. Instead she'd moved in here quietly, with no discussion. She didn't mention it, and she hadn't heard David complain.

She smoothed out the quilt, then lay down and tucked herself in. As soon as her head hit the pillow, her eyes closed. This was the end of another long day in a week of long days, and she was beyond exhausted. Too many meetings at work, too much stress at home, and, of course, there was the pregnancy fatigue on top of it all.

But, of course, now she couldn't sleep. Fluffing up her pillow, rearranging the covers, turning over and over—nothing helped. Her mind wouldn't stop racing. Lying there with the quilt pulled up to her chin, she simply gazed out the window, at the inky sky dotted with stars. The moon shone bright and full, and in the back of her mind she heard the ocean, smelled the salty air and the tropical flowers. She felt the brush of Michael's damp skin against hers.

A part of her felt like she would never get off of that island, would never stop thinking about the memories of that time and place. She seemed to return to it again and again, every time she was stressed out, when she was missing Michael, when she was simply tired of it all. Whenever she wanted to get away and start over, the echo of the waves returned to her, beckoning her away from life as she knew it and into the great, amazing unknown.

With a sigh she picked up her cell phone and checked her email. Nothing but work messages. She scrolled back through her text messages from throughout the day—Michael was always checking on her and the baby or just letting her know he was thinking about them. Carolina smiled as she read them. Everything Michael wrote warmed her heart.

Yawning wide, she closed her eyes again, finally thinking she might be able to get some sleep. *Would be nice to have a good dream*, she thought, more visions of Michael running through her mind—his lips, his hands, what he could do with them...

And then her phone buzzed. Carolina opened her eyes. She wanted to be mad, but she couldn't. She knew it was Michael.

Come outside, the message read.

She looked at it for a moment. *What do you mean, Michael?* she replied. *I'm in bed. Is everything okay? Where are you?*

A few moments passed. Carolina thought about getting up to look out the window, but the fatigue was overwhelming her. That's how it happened with pregnancy—one minute sleepless, the next ready to pass out. The phone buzzed again.

I mean come outside, Carolina. I'm out here waiting for you.

Well, now she had to get up and look. She threw back the covers and put her feet on the floor—slowly, though. It was still early in her pregnancy, but every now and again she'd have a dizzy spell. She wanted to jump out of bed and run to the window, but knew it wasn't the safest thing to do. Instead she stood up slowly and scurried across the room.

At the window she pulled back the sheer curtain. Outside, the street was quiet and calm. It was late, and all her neighbors were asleep. A huge tree blocked her view of almost everything—an enormous, old weeping willow they'd had in the front yard for ages. It was in full bloom at the moment, and its green leaves raked slightly against one another in the breeze, making a *shh-shh* sound that Carolina loved. She bent down a little, trying to see under its low-hanging boughs, and spied nothing out of the ordinary.

And then her heart skipped a beat. There, directly underneath the tree and a little bit behind it, she could just see the corner of a car. Black, headlights off but parking lights on, windshield wipers intermittently clearing the glass of a fine, light mist that fell from the sky.

It was Michael's car. He really was there. What could have happened? Why would he do this? Her heart skipped a beat. Forgetting completely about the dizziness, she ran quickly out of the room and down the hallway, padding along on her bare feet, trying to be careful not to wake up anyone else. Downstairs, the first floor was completely silent. She felt like a cat burglar in her own house, sneaking around in the middle of the night while everyone slept.

In the foyer she opened the closet and pulled out her coat, then slipped it on over her pink silk pajamas and tied its belt. Crouching down, she rummaged around in the bottom of the closet for a moment and came out with her running shoes. She put them on her feet and headed out the door.

On the porch, the cool night air hit her full in the face, and she stopped for a moment. The rain was falling harder now—not a storm yet, but more than a drizzle. She looked out toward the street, at the corner of Michael's car. The windows were dark, not even the glow of his cell phone to light the inside.

It was all she could do not to run all the way down the steps.

At the door of the car she paused again, her heart beating fast. She felt so afraid—that he would be hurt, that he would have bad news of some sort. Why else would he show up at her house, unannounced, so late at night? Standing there with her fingers on the door handle, the rain hitting her face, she tried to will herself to open the door.

Just do it, she thought. *Just get in and get it over with.*

"Get in," Michael said. Suddenly he was standing behind her. "You're all wet. I don't want you to get sick."

Reaching around her to grab the handle of the door, Michael pressed his body against her back for a moment. Carolina closed her eyes. He was so warm, so inviting. She wanted to turn and bury her face in his chest, slip her arms inside his coat and around his waist.

"Go ahead," he urged her patiently, holding the door open. "Get in and get warm."

Carolina did as she was told, curling her body onto the comfy leather seat. In a flash Michael was back in the car, seated beside her. Before he said anything, he put his hands on her face and kissed her. Long and slow, taking his time, as if there were nothing else in the world he wanted to do. Like nothing existed outside of this car. And for Carolina, in that moment, nothing did. It was just her and him again, as it always had been, as it always would be. How she had waited for this; how she'd longed for it. Now that it was here, she didn't want it to end.

Michael sat back, then reached up to the dashboard and aimed the heating vents toward her. "Are you warm enough?" he asked, taking her hands in his and rubbing them.

Carolina laughed. "I'm fine, Michael. I was only out there for a minute."

He looked at her, his face serious. "But you have to take care of yourself." He looked at her belly for a moment, then reached over and put his palm flat against it. "And I'll take care of both of you."

Carolina kissed him again. She couldn't help it. She loved how he loved her, how he was there for her. With Michael she didn't have to be in control all the time. That was a change for her—but she was finding that she liked it. She'd never let anyone take care of her, but she was eager to try.

"What are you doing here?" she asked him at last.

"I'm sorry, I know it's late. But I just had to tell you."

Carolina smiled at him, enjoying the mystery of this meeting. "Tell me what?" she asked, putting a hand up to his face.

Michael turned in his seat a little further, until he was almost facing the backseat. Then he brought his hand up and switched on the light. Carolina turned too and looked in the back. She saw a stack of black suitcases, three in all, and a duffel bag on top. On the hook by the window hung a garment bag, the collar of a suit jacket peeking out the top.

She looked back at him. "Michael," she said. "What is all this?"

"It's my clothes," he replied, a bit of a smile on his face. "There's two more in the trunk, too. I didn't know I had so much to wear."

They gazed at each other for a moment, that magnetic feeling coming over them again—that hypnotism they always felt whenever they looked deeply into one another's eyes. In these moments, Carolina could see everything between them, could actually feel the bond that held them together. Tonight it was stronger than ever, and she knew it would only increase. She also knew, when she looked into his eyes, what he was thinking, just as he always seemed to know what was on her mind.

And at that moment, everything became clear to her.

"Michael," she whispered, her eyes wide. "You left."

Michael nodded as if in a daze. "Yeah," he replied, reaching out to run his hand through her hair. The touch, it seemed, brought him back to life. He shook his head a little and his focus returned to the present. "I'm going to stay at my sister's for a while."

"Oh, Michael," Carolina said, leaning over to put her arms around him. She wasn't sure whether to comfort him or celebrate; her heart wanted to cheer, but she knew this was a difficult situation for him. This meant they could be together now, but it also meant the end of his marriage and major changes in his relationships with his children. Neither of those was anything worth cheering about.

"What can I do?" she whispered in his ear, then moved her lips down to kiss his neck. He was so warm, his body so inviting, once again she fought the urge just to press herself against him, to climb onto his lap and nestle in.

"You've already done everything," he said back to her, his voice low. He kissed her forehead. "Just being with me is enough. You're having my baby. I couldn't ask for anything more than that from anyone."

Carolina sat up straight again and looked at him. "But you can," she reassured him. "Anything you need, anytime." She did reach inside his coat now and put a hand on his chest. She felt his heart beating, so warm and alive. "I'm completely yours, and you're completely mine. It took us over forty years to find each other, and now until eternity we'll be together, Michael. We're finally, really together. We're all we have to rely on from now on."

"You and me," Michael repeated, and suddenly he began to cry. In a moment tears streamed down his cheeks.

"It's okay," Carolina told him gently. "It's okay."

Michael nodded, sniffling and wiping at his eyes with the back of his hand. He managed a laugh. "I know, everything is okay. I...I just can't believe it. I've never felt like this before, Carolina. Not in a long time. I can't believe I finally feel...so free, like a huge weight has just been lifted."

He laughed again, this time more loudly, and hit his hand against the steering wheel. He looked at Carolina. "It's really over," he said, and the relief in his voice was tangible.

Carolina smiled, clasping her hands together in front of her mouth, trying not to break out in tears of joy herself. "No, babe," she said. "It's really just beginning."

Part Two

Twelve

Carolina loved being pregnant. No, it was more than that: she loved carrying Michael's child.

There was always something magical about having a baby. She'd felt it with her first three, a sort of glow and a hum all over her body, a rush of strong emotions that never seemed to end. But with this one it was different. The feeling was stronger somehow, and more intense. Maybe it was because this baby had been conceived unexpectedly, or maybe it was because she'd never thought she'd have a baby again. Something about renewed hope, renewed life—a second chance. That was what this baby and Michael gave her.

Now that she was starting the second trimester—*Already!* she thought as she realized it, almost not believing the time had passed so quickly—she'd decided to take it easy at work, go in only a few days a week and keep her hours short. There was so much to do, aside from the napping and eating, both of which she did like they were her full-time job. She had to think about her birth plan, and focus on the nursery, and, of course, spend as much one-on-one time with Michael as she could. Soon they wouldn't be alone anymore; instead of making love into the small hours of the morning or staying up talking, there would be midnight diaper changes and 2:00 a.m. feedings. Being parents again would suck every ounce of energy out of them, no question, and Carolina was worried they wouldn't have time for one another anymore, so until that day came, she made sure to savor every moment with him. She made him breakfast in the morning and rubbed his back when he got home from work at night, and lured him into the bedroom as often as possible. Not surprisingly, that wasn't a difficult task at all.

Examining a collection of paint swatches, Carolina held a couple up to the wall of the baby's room, looking for the perfect color combination. Since they didn't know if they were having a boy or a girl, it had to be a neutral color, just to be safe. The man at the paint store had recommended a number of pleasing yellows, but Carolina was leaning more toward a pale celery green. Something about it was just so fresh, so serene—it felt right to her. And more than ever now, she was beginning to trust her gut instinct.

"It's gotten me this far," she said to herself absently, considering an antique white for the trim. She smiled. "And it certainly hasn't steered me wrong."

Across the room, on the window sill, her cell phone buzzed, beckoning her to answer it. Carolina ignored it for a moment, still rearranging the paint chips in her hand, trying to make that perfect match pop out at her. When the phone buzzed again she stuck out her lower lip and blew her hair out of her face, then marched over to see who was sending her messages. Even her bare feet made a loud sound, her steps echoing off the naked walls. She picked up the phone.

Hello, beautiful, read the first message. *Just checking in. How are you feeling? Have you picked a color yet? Wish I could be there with you. Can't wait to get home to the love of my life—the two loves of my life.*

Carolina smiled, feeling a little guilty now about playing hooky so often. Michael continually worked so hard, and she was used to doing the same. She felt like she should contribute more. Gazing out the window, she ran a hand down her softly bulging belly and reminded herself—as Michael always did—that she was doing enough. Her assistants and coworkers were perfectly capable of handling everything at the office, and she could work from home if she needed to. Mostly importantly, she needed to rest. She also needed to make this house they'd bought into a home in preparation for the addition to the family to come.

Before answering Michael's message, she slowly scrolled through the rest of her messages to see if she'd missed any. Michael, Michael, Michael—he was the only one who texted her regularly, and she'd read every message that he'd sent. Then she stopped short. That second buzz she'd heard, it hadn't been a message from Michael. It was from her son, Patrick. She stared at his name for a moment, almost afraid of what the message might say. The breakup of her marriage, it seemed, had affected him the most. The girls had taken it okay; they'd even come over to the new house and picked out their bedrooms, where they would stay whenever they came over. Patrick had come too, and had met Michael on quite a few occasions, as had the girls. They'd all gotten along fine—even better than Carolina had thought they would under the circumstances.

But it had been a rough three months since she'd moved out. Tough for her, and especially tough for her son. At almost eighteen, he was old enough to understand exactly what was going on between his parents; he was practically a man but still enough of a child to feel the sting of their breakup. He loved Carolina, that she knew, but he loved his father equally, and if David was hurting, Patrick undoubtedly was as well. He was in a precarious place, and Carolina just wasn't sure how to handle it.

"Well, you can start by answering him," she told herself. If Patrick needed to talk, she'd drop everything in a minute. She loved that boy, and she never meant to disrupt his life and never wanted to disappoint him. No matter what he had to say, Carolina had to deal with it. Good or bad, she had to help him see it through.

With a deep breath, she opened his message, preparing herself for whatever he had to say. *Mom*, it read, *do you think you'll be able to make my game on Saturday?*

Carolina smiled big, her hand automatically going up to her heart, trying to calm the fluttering inside her chest. She hadn't expected that message; in fact she'd thought it would be just the opposite. She'd thought he might show anger, or at least disappointment, and deep down she felt like she would have deserved it. But to see that simple question, one he'd asked her a hundred times in the past while she and David were still together…that gave her hope. It showed he still wanted his mother in his life.

Wouldn't miss it for the world, she wrote back. *In fact I'll even give you a ride. What time can I pick you up?*

Pausing, Carolina waited for his answer. She leaned against the window frame and looked out on the backyard again. This one was nothing like the yard she and David created at her old house—no manicured lawn, no Japanese maples, nothing that required a lot of maintenance. Just some sod and a few overgrown rose bushes, that was about it. She loved her old yard and her old house and had so many good memories of the times she had spent there with her family. But this was a new place, a new time, a new phase of her life. This home had to be different; it had to be more reflective of herself and Michael.

The house she and David owned was all about order, about the control she'd always tried to impose on everything. That was how she'd been for the last twenty years, in a mad dash to keep the world from spinning out of control. Now, with Michael, she could see it was okay to let go of the reins once in a while. To let things get messy. To enjoy a little chaos. Their whole relationship so far had been the definition of a whirlwind, and she'd loved every minute of it. Michael had taught her how to stop and smell the roses, how to live life to its fullest. All she wanted at this point was to enjoy every minute with the one man she truly loved and the child who would complete them.

A new text message came in from Patrick. *Sounds great*, he wrote. *Pick me up at noon.*

Can't wait to see you, she replied. *I've missed you. XOXO.* There was so much more she wanted to say to him, but she didn't want to overdo it. Too much from her and he might back away just when he was making an effort to get close.

The phone buzzed back immediately. *I love you too, Mom.*

"Love you too, baby," Carolina whispered, saving the message so she would never lose it, so she would always have it to remind her. Then, leaving her paint swatches on the window sill, she took her phone and headed downstairs to the kitchen. It was already lunchtime, and the baby was sure letting her know.

"Never miss a meal, do you?" she said with a laugh as she opened the refrigerator and examined what was inside. Leftovers, fruits, vegetables...unsure what she wanted, she grabbed an armload and carted it to the table. Setting it down along with her phone, she sat on a chair and looked at what she'd brought. Picking out an apple from the bunch, she sunk her teeth into it, savoring its crispness and tangy bite.

"Oh," she said with her mouth full, just remembering she owed a text message to Michael. She pulled her phone out and started typing.

I'm doing great, better than ever now. I just received a text message from Patrick, can't wait to tell you about it later. Miss you. Xoxo.

Eying a package of cheese, Carolina tore it open and cut a large slice. As she ate it, she looked around the kitchen, making mental notes: more pot lights over the sink, change the backsplash tiles behind the stove, maybe add an island...

No, she thought. That would make it look too much like her old home—David's home now. Well, it was still hers in a way; she still had some equity although she no longer lived there. But for all intents and purposes *this* home was her home now, her home with Michael. This was where her lifelong dream was coming true—to be with her soul mate, her one true love, to build a life with this man and raise their child together.

She paused for a moment. It was happening. It was really happening. Everything she'd imagined, all that she'd hoped for... So, why did she still feel so conflicted?

Her phone rang, drawing her out of the dark ruminations that threatened to take over her mind. She picked it up from the table and looked at the screen. A picture of Alexis beamed out at her, smiling from ear to ear. Her caller ID picture. Carolina's heart skipped a beat.

"Hello, sweetheart!" she answered, the joy she felt at hearing from her daughter coming through. "How are you?"

"I'm good, Mommy," Alexis said, her little-girl voice sounding small and far away. Just the thought of the distance between them almost brought Carolina to tears. "What are you doing?"

"Well, I'm eating lunch right now. What are you doing?"

"Playing with Patrick." Carolina listened close and could hear the sounds of a video game in the background. She hoped it wasn't one of those violent shoot-'em-up things that he liked.

"Sounds like fun," she said. "So what's going on?"

It wasn't rare for Alexis to call her—she did so at least once a day—but when she did, it was always with a question, or a statement, or a problem. Alexis was a focused child—another trait Carolina had passed along to her. She wondered what was on her youngest child's mind at the moment.

"Well, I was thinking," Alexis said, but then she trailed off. Carolina heard fake gunfire.

"Alexis, what are you playing?" she asked, trying her best to sound stern, but just a little bit. She was still figuring out where her authority lay now that she no longer lived with her children, and she didn't want to overstep any boundaries.

"Nothing," came the quick reply, then there was a shuffle, as if Alexis were getting up and moving. Carolina heard a door close, and the sounds of the game disappeared. "I was just thinking."

"About what, sweetie?" Phone in one hand, Carolina sifted with the other through the pile of food on the table. She found a bag of grapes and popped a few in her mouth.

"About coming to live with you and Michael in your house."

Carolina stopped mid-chew. She felt like a bomb had just dropped. All of a sudden it seemed like the wind outside had ceased to blow, like the silence in the house had become a scream. Had she heard her daughter right? No, she couldn't have. After all she had put her children through, there was no way any of them would choose to come and live with her. Sure, she'd thought about it; in fact, she'd dreamed about it. And she had thought maybe, down the line—but *years* down the line. It had only been a few months since she'd left, only a matter of weeks since her divorce from David had become final.

"Say that again, sweetie?" she asked, pressing the phone in harder against her ear.

"I said I want to come live with you!" Alexis whispered loudly, as if she were trying not to let anyone else hear.

Carolina swallowed hard. "Well, hmmm..." She stopped and cleared her throat, unsure exactly what she should say. Of course, she wanted to scream, "Yes! We'll see about this weekend!" But she knew this decision wouldn't be entirely up to her. There would be discussions and negotiations—with David and with Michael. She didn't even know if either one would consider it, David especially. They did have joint custody, fifty-fifty, as a part of their divorce settlement. But they both knew the kids would stay with him so their lives wouldn't be uprooted. It was probably better that way. Or so they'd thought. Apparently, Alexis had other ideas.

And now, Carolina had some ideas of her own.

Thirteen

You busy? Can we talk?

Michael read Carolina's message as he walked into his office. After closing the door, he took off his white coat and tossed it onto the back of a chair. Settling in behind his desk, he put his feet up and just sat there for a moment. It had been a long, busy morning already. He'd been on his feet since he got out of bed.

I have a few—he started to type but then was interrupted by the ring of his office phone. He backspaced. *Have to take a call, then I'll get back to you. Love you*, he replied, then leaned over to pick up the other phone.

"Dr. Sanford," he said, swinging his chair around to look out the window. Another cloudy day with rain on the horizon. On days like this he still recalled that private little island, the one he'd escaped to with Carolina. It had been only three months ago, but it seemed a lifetime away. He had to struggle to remember what the sun felt like on his skin.

"Hey, Dad!" his daughter greeted him. "Are you busy?"

Michael sat up straight and turned back to his desk. He leaned his elbows on the blotter and pressed the phone intently to his hear. "Never too busy for you, sweetheart," he said, a big smile growing across his face. It felt so good to hear Emily's bubbly voice. That had never changed—she always sounded happy to talk to him. Though Julie had predicted differently, his relationships with his children had remained as strong as ever. Michael was incredibly thankful for that. "What's going on?"

"Oh, nothing. Just wanted to say hi and see how you're doing. How's the new house coming?"

"It's looking good. Carolina's doing a great job," he replied, impressed by his daughter's easy interest in the details of his new life. "Ordered some new furniture, getting everything set up. You'd really love it. It's a great house."

"Can't wait to see it," she replied. "Working on my room yet?"

"Not without your consent," Michael said with a laugh. He knew better than to try to decorate a teenage girl's room all by himself. Even Carolina refused to take part in the task until Emily gave some idea of what her tastes were.

"How about—" he began, but suddenly stopped himself. *How about we go shopping next weekend*, he was about to say, *to buy some things to decorate your room?* But that wasn't possible. Julie wouldn't let her go. At that point, Julie wouldn't even allow Emily to get within a hundred yards of Michael. He hadn't seen her or his son since the day he'd moved out of the house. They hadn't even met Carolina, hadn't seen the rooms Michael had picked out for them. Julie wouldn't let them.

You are not seeing your father, he could hear his ex-wife yelling. *He's hurt our family, he's hurt me. I forbid you to see him—ever!*

"How's Carolina, Dad?" Emily asked, breaking into his thoughts, as if she knew from the silence what he'd been thinking about. "How's my future brother or sister?"

These simple questions made Michael's heart ache and at the same time made his chest swell up with pride. Emily was so accepting and understanding of the entire situation. Not surprising, Michael realized, considering what she'd seen. For years Emily and her brother had been witnesses to their parents' failing marriage, had watched and listened as it crashed and burned even as Michael and Julie had tried to hide it from them. Michael was amazed by how well his daughter had come out of it; she was smart, funny, optimistic, kind, and compassionate, all the things a father hoped his child would be.

"They're both doing well, thanks," he said, once again smiling. "Just going through normal pregnancy stuff, but everything's going along just as it should be."

"Cool." In the background Michael heard some noises—kids yelling and lockers slamming, a crowded high school hallway. "Listen, Dad, I'm on lunch break, and I have to get back to class now." Her voice was hesitant. "Can I call you tonight?"

Michael didn't like the doubt he heard in his young daughter's voice, the notes of sadness and loneliness he wished he couldn't detect. "Of course you can, sweetheart. Anytime. I'm always here for you."

Emily paused. In the distance Michael heard someone calling her. "I know you are, Dad. I'm here for you too, you know. I love you. Talk to you soon." And with a click, she was gone.

Michael sat for a few minutes, just holding the phone receiver in his hand. He looked blankly around his office, at the furniture, the shelves lined with his medical books, the curtains on the windows. *We fill our lives with things*, he mused, *but we can't be with the people who matter to us most.* It didn't seem right; it definitely wasn't fair.

"Then why aren't you *doing* something about it?" he asked himself as he slammed the phone back into the receiver. That had to change immediately. There was no good reason for this game Julie was playing, and he had to put an end to it. As much as he didn't want to call a lawyer on her, it was the only option at this point. She wouldn't budge. There was no alternative.

He would call his attorney first thing in the morning. Enough was enough. He had to get his children back into his life.

With a heavy sigh, Michael rubbed his temples. The stress was weighing on him. Through everything, he'd treated Julia with nothing but respect; he knew he was the bad guy in this situation and so he deferred to whatever she said or told him to do. To take his mind off things, he threw himself into his work—staying busy was his out, almost the only way to keep his sanity. Or, at least, that was how it used to be. Now he had a bigger reason—two, actually: Carolina and the baby.

He thought about them all afternoon as he examined his patients. He was anxious to get home, to enfold himself in the sanctuary of Carolina's arms. When he eventually got there, it was after dark but still early enough to enjoy some time with the one woman he couldn't live without. Dinner, conversation—to Michael, that was the perfect evening.

But when he arrived home he found Carolina in bed. The house was dark, and she was sound asleep. She barely moved as he sat down beside her and lifted the covers.

"Michael," she moaned, not even opening her eyes. "What time is it?" She sounded groggy, and immediately Michael began to worry. He picked up her wrist and felt her pulse. Not the strongest he'd ever felt it, but not weak either. He put a hand to her forehead.

"Are you not feeling well, babe?" he asked her. "Do you ache anywhere? Pain? Do you feel cold? Do you have chills? A fever?"

Carolina smiled at him weakly, reaching up to grab his hand from her head. She brought it down to her lips and kissed it. "I'm fine, although I must say I love having my own personal doctor," she whispered, pulling his arm to make him get into bed with her. He took the hint, kicked off his shoes, and slid in beside her, working his arms tightly around her small frame.

"Are you sure you're okay?" he asked, putting a hand to her abdomen. He pressed on it gently with his fingertips.

Carolina winced a little; the touch hurt, but she tried not to show it. "Yes, I'm sure," she said, moving his hand away. "Just a few little cramps, that's all. I had to lie down for a while."

"Alright," Michael said, then kissed the top of her head. "But promise me you'll let me know if it happens again?"

"Promise." Carolina laid her head on his chest, her hand reaching around to his side. "Now, how was your day, sweetheart?"

"Same as usual," Michael replied, willing his body to relax. "Emily called. It was really good to hear from her."

Carolina looked up at him. "Alexis called too." She smiled. "Guess our daughters are thinking about us today."

"Mmm," Michael agreed, closing his eyes. "How's she doing?"

"Good," Carolina said. She paused, as if thinking about what she wanted to say. "Michael, Alexis said something to me—"

He opened his eyes again. He raised his brows at Carolina, urging her to go on.

"Well, she... I'm not certain why she said this, but...she wants to come live with us."

Michael was silent for a moment. "Just Alexis? Not Patrick or Lindsay? Why not all three?" He sat up, a smile spreading across his face. "Hey, how about all *five*? That would be great!" He thought about it—a house full of children. What a visual. Full of noise, full of laughter…what a wonderful home that would be.

"Yes, it would," Carolina agreed, shifting slowly under the covers until she was sitting up. "And you know it could happen… While Alexis was talking to me, Lindsay grabbed the phone and said she wanted to come too." She looked at him expectantly. "What do you think, Michael? I guess as long as David agrees… I know he'd be lonely without them, but other than that, I don't know why he'd say no. We live close enough—the girls could visit him often."

Michael looked at her. He reached out to tuck her long hair behind her ear. Even half asleep, with no makeup, Carolina was the most beautiful woman ever to walk on this earth. *How did I get so lucky?* he thought to himself. *And how could I deny her anything?*

"I think it's a great idea," he concluded. "Let's do it. The sooner the better."

With a happy laugh, Carolina lunged at Michael and threw her arms around his shoulders. She kissed every inch of his face and squeezed him tight, then sat back again. "Thank you, Michael," she said, clasping her hands in front of her, a hopeful pose. "Thank you so much. You have no idea what this means to me."

"You don't have to thank me, babe," he said, shaking his head. "I'd love to have them here, honestly. They're your children—they're wonderful, just like you are." He closed his eyes, once again visualizing a happy, crowded home. Just the way it was meant to be. He couldn't wait to make it happen.

Just then, Carolina screamed in extreme pain…

Fourteen

Carolina's obstetrician was wonderful, but the chairs in the waiting room were uncomfortable. She shifted her weight from side to side as she sat, crossing and uncrossing her legs at the ankles, trying to find some type of comforting position. So far, she'd had no such luck.

"Are you alright?" Michael asked immediately, seeing her discomfort. Sitting next to her, he reached over and rubbed her back, hoping it would help her feel more at ease.

Carolina smiled at him. He asked her that same question about every five minutes lately. Sometimes—when those hormones got a hold of her—it occasionally annoyed her. But she knew that was irrational. Most of the time, and especially right now, she adored it. Michael was so attentive to her needs and to the baby's. There was nothing he wouldn't do for either one of them.

"I'm just fine," she reassured him, putting a hand on his knee and rubbing it. "Just trying to get comfortable."

"Are you nervous?"

Carolina looked around the room, at the other expectant mothers. There was a redhead with a huge baby bump, probably due at any moment. A younger woman with a smaller belly ran around after her other child, a very active toddler. Carolina smiled—she remembered those days. There weren't big gaps between her children's ages. With Patrick and Lindsay, one was barely out of diapers before the other arrived.

"Not at all," she said, her mind drifting back to when her children were younger. She thought of Patrick's sweet face the first time she saw it, when the doctor placed him on her chest after his birth. He was her firstborn, and she'd been so enchanted with him—still was, truth be told. Of course, she didn't play favorites; she loved each of her wonderful children equally. But she had a bond with her son that was different from what she had with her daughters. Not because he was a boy but because her pregnancy with him was a new experience for her. It had been beautiful and amazing. She would never forget it. She would always remember that time in her life no matter what fate might bring her in the future.

"Carolina, the doctor will see you now." A nurse in pink scrubs poked her head out of the door and beckoned her back into the exam area. Carolina clutched the arm of her chair and prepared to push herself out of it, but before she could make a move, Michael was on his feet. He wrapped his strong hands around her arms and slowly lifted her up.

"Easy," he whispered to her, a look of intense concentration on his face. "Take it slow now."

When she stood at her full height—plus a little; she wasn't ready to give up her heels just yet—she leaned in and kissed Michael quickly. "Thanks, babe," she said with a smirk, dragging her thumb across his mouth to rub off the lipstick smudge she'd left. "But I'm fine, Michael. I'm only twenty weeks pregnant. I'm still able to haul myself out of a chair—for now. Wait another few months and you'll need a rope to hoist me up off the sofa."

Michael smiled at her and laughed a little. That was his Carolina—independent to the core. He knew she loved it when he helped her and when he took care of her. He could see it in her eyes and feel it in the way her body responded to his touch. She always softened for him, always let her guard down and let him guide her or hold her or whatever she happened to need him to do. But there would always be that streak in her—she would always do for herself first, before asking him or anyone else for assistance. And he loved that about her. She was her own woman, strong and tough and beautiful. He wouldn't want her any other way.

"How are you feeling?" the nurse asked Carolina with a smile as she and Michael headed through the doorway. The nurse showed her to a chair and put a blood pressure cuff on her arm.

"Feeling great now," Carolina replied. "Really great." And it was true. No morning sickness, a little tired, of course, and she had occasional painful cramping. But otherwise this pregnancy was a breeze. "I wish my first three had been so easy."

The nurse smiled. "Oh, you have other children?" she asked, her gaze darting back and forth between Carolina and Michael, suggesting the already-existing family belonged to both of them.

"Uh, no," Carolina said, glancing at Michael as well. He winked at her, letting her know the question didn't bother him. She turned back to the nurse. "I mean, yes, we both have children from previous marriages. This is our first together."

The nurse took off the cuff. "Well, that's wonderful. And so is your blood pressure. One ten over seventy. Now if you'll follow me..."

Carolina rose—again with Michael's help, which he insisted on giving—and followed the nurse down a hallway and into a room. The nurse gave her a gown and dimmed the lights a little, then left the two alone. Carolina changed and let Michael help her up onto the exam table. As she lay down, she shivered a little; the room was cold. For the first time, she had to admit, she felt a pang of anxiety.

Turning her head toward Michael, she reached out and took him by the hand. "Are *you* nervous?" she asked him, looking deeply into his eyes. They stayed just like that for a moment, letting their connection flow through them both. Carolina felt the old familiar pull, the magnetism that always held her to him. The sensation comforted her; it let her know she was exactly where she was meant to be and that everything would be okay.

"Not one bit," Michael whispered to her, then leaned in to give her a slow, gentle kiss, just the kind she needed right then. She closed her eyes and savored it, forgetting all about the cold room, the flimsy gown, the ultrasound machine humming right alongside them. Michael pulled back a little bit and grinned at her. "I can't wait to see our baby again."

Carolina smiled too. They'd had a few sonograms by then, and Michael had been there for them. He'd gone to every appointment with her, even if they were just routine checkups. He wanted to show her—to make sure she really knew—she was not alone in this. She might have been carrying their child, but he was there with her every step of the way.

He had to be. He had wanted this child from the moment he knew it existed and had gone to such lengths to get Carolina to feel the same way. He couldn't back off now. What's more, he didn't want to. This all was such a miracle—not just the baby but their whole life together. That they'd made a home together, that they'd conceived a child, that they'd even met at all. It was all so improbable. Most days Michael could hardly believe any of it had happened.

But it had. And he was so grateful. And he would do anything to show Carolina just how much it all meant to him.

"Good afternoon," the doctor said as she came into the room, looking down at Carolina's chart. When she reached the ultrasound machine, she stopped and looked up at them. She smiled. "How are we doing?"

Michael straightened up but didn't let go of Carolina's hand. "We're doing great," he said to the doctor, his eyes still on Carolina. "But I should probably let the mommy be the one to tell you all about it."

"I have a better idea," the doctor said with a laugh as she pulled the ultrasound wand from its holder on the machine. "How about we let the baby tell us?"

Michael and Carolina grinned at one another, the anticipation of seeing their child sending an electric feeling through them both.

"Sounds good to me," Carolina said, reaching down to open her gown. The doctor squeezed some gel onto the wand, then gently placed it on Carolina's slightly rounded belly. The gel was cold, and Carolina flinched. Michael squeezed her hand as they both turned their attention to the screen.

"First we'll listen to the heartbeat," the doctor said as she moved the wand around, below and a little to the right of Carolina's navel. Soon they could hear it—the strong, steady *whoosh, whoosh, whoosh* of the baby's heartbeat. Michael laughed, and Carolina's eyes filled with tears. What a relief it always was to hear that beautiful sound.

"Sounds good," the doctor said. "Now let's check out that anatomy." As she slid the wand around over Carolina's skin, she spoke calmly and quietly, keeping them informed of what she was doing. "As you know, at twenty weeks gestation we go a little more in depth with the ultrasound so we can check the baby's physical growth and see how he or she is progressing. We'll take some measurements and if we're lucky, you'll get to—oh, look at that!"

Carolina raised her head a little, and Michael leaned over her to see the screen. The doctor raised a finger and pointed at the image there, black and white and fuzzy but unmistakably—

"That's the baby's face!" Carolina whispered. She turned to Michael. "Do you see it? It's staring directly at both of us!"

Michael had a hand up to his mouth. His eyes were wide. He nodded his head slowly. "I see it," he said, his voice full of very genuine awe. "I see it." He leaned over a little more, pressing his finger against the glass of the monitor. "There's the eyes, and the nose…"

He stayed that way for a moment, running his fingertip across the likeness of his child. The room was silent; no one even dared to breathe. Then, just as quickly as the baby's face had come into view, it disappeared. The baby turned, and the glimpse they'd had was gone.

The doctor laughed. "That's an active little one you have there!" She continued moving the ultrasound wand up and down, trying to get a good image of the baby's head size. "We don't always get to see a baby's face in an ultrasound. All depends if they're facing the right way. You two got lucky today."

"We sure did," Michael said as he drew his hand away and slipped it back into Carolina's. He gazed down at her, and she could see on his face the way he felt: awed, inspired, full of wonder. "Did you see that?" he asked her. "Her face…or *his* face…that was amazing. I saw it so clearly."

Carolina nodded. "I saw it too, babe. It was amazing. Our baby is beautiful."

Turning back to the monitor, Carolina watched as the doctor went through her routine, measuring the baby's arms and legs, its length from head to feet. Every time she showed something new on the monitor—some blurry toes, a wave of a hand—she stopped and pointed it out, giving Michael and Carolina all the time they wanted to look at their child. This was the best view they'd gotten of the little one yet.

"Well, now," the doctor said at last, pulling the ultrasound wand back from Carolina's stomach. "There's something here we have to discuss." She looked at both of the expectant parents, her face very serious. Carolina and Michael both held their breath, unsure what the doctor was going to say. Was something wrong? Had she seen something abnormal in the ultrasound? Carolina had been watching it carefully, and she knew Michael had too, but in reality it was all a little confusing to her. She could see her baby's outline, but that was it. Was there a fine detail, a measurement here or a shadow there, that wasn't quite right?

Please let our baby be okay! Carolina quickly prayed, her heart doing flip-flops in her chest. She looked up at Michael, and he looked at her too; she could tell he was just as worried as she was. He brought her hand up to his mouth and kissed it, then clutched it closely in front of his chest.

Then the doctor broke out into a smile. "Relax, you guys. I just thought I'd ask if you want to know the baby's sex. Do you want to know if it's a boy or a girl?"

Carolina and Michael both exhaled loudly.

"Oh, God," Michael said with a bit of a laugh. He brought up a hand and wiped it across his forehead. "You had me going there for a minute." He shook a finger at the doctor, good-naturedly admonishing her. "You got me. I thought something was wrong with the baby."

The doctor shook her head vigorously. "No, no, I'm so sorry. I didn't mean that at all. I'm sorry it came out that way." She looked at Carolina then and smiled. "Don't worry, Mom, everything's okay! The measurements are good, lots of movement on the baby's part, everything is going just as it should be."

Carolina nodded at her. "Thank you, Doctor. You really did scare me for a minute. You know, I worry—I haven't had a baby in years, and I'm a little older now—"

The doctor waved a hand at her. "Oh, don't spend another minute thinking that. You're in perfect health and I have no doubt your pregnancy and your baby will be just fine. God's the only one who knows for sure. Now," she said, poising the wand back over Carolina's belly, her eyebrows raised, "do you want to know if you're having a son or a daughter?"

Carolina looked at Michael. In the dimness of the room, everything about him looked so soft to her—his hair, his skin, his eyes. He looked so peaceful, so glowing in the almost-darkness. "What do you think?" she asked him, reaching up to brush her hand against his cheek.

He leaned into the touch and closed his eyes for a moment. He took a deep breath and thought about it. For a while he'd thought he would want to find out, thought that knowing the gender of their baby would make things easier—the planning, the decorating, the shopping for clothes and supplies. Besides, it would be nice to be able to say "him" or "her" instead of "it." He and Carolina had talked about it a few times, but never at length, and they'd never really come to a conclusion. Now they had to. And all he could think was—

"No." He opened his eyes, surprising even himself with the answer that had come out of his mouth. "Carolina, I don't want to know. I want to be surprised. Do you?"

Carolina still looked up at him, her eyes sparkling wildly in the low light. Michael reached down to touch her too, to feel the soft silkiness of her hair. For a moment it was as if they were alone in the room, as if the doctor weren't even there. Just them and the baby, the three of them, as it was now and as it always would be.

As it's supposed to be, Carolina thought. She wondered how she ever could have doubted her desire to have a baby with this wonderful man.

"Yes," she replied then, turning her attention back to the doctor. "I mean no. We don't want to know."

"Oh!" the doctor said, pulling the wand back quickly. "Well, that's unusual. Everyone wants to know these days." She holstered the wand again and pressed a button, and a series of pictures from the ultrasound began to print. "May I ask why you decided that?"

Once again Carolina and Michael looked at each other. Their eyes locked. How could they explain it? How could they explain anything that had happened to them up to this point?

"Just seems like the right thing to do," Michael said softly, never taking his eyes off of Carolina's face. "I can't tell you. I just know this is how it's supposed to be."

Fifteen

Seven o'clock, end of the shift. Michael should have been hanging up his stethoscope and waving goodbye to the nurses, checking himself out of the staff parking garage and heading home. But he wasn't even close to that. He still had patients to see, paperwork to do, and orders to follow up on. At least a couple hours' worth—or maybe more. When he was at the hospital, he rarely kept track of time.

"Mr. Gurman," he said as he entered the room of a patient, an older man who'd just undergone a triple bypass. Though Michael hadn't done the surgery, as the man's GP it was his job to check up on his aftercare. Michael looked at his chart, then headed to the bedside. He smiled at the man; often, he found, a little good cheer could make all the difference. "How are you feeling tonight?"

The gray-haired man smiled too. "Better than last night," he said, his voice hoarse and weak. "Thanks to my cardiologist and you, Doctor."

Michael reached for the man's wrist to check on his pulse. He was used to this—so many of his patients praised him for the work that he did. He appreciated it, but he never let it go to his head. He was in this line of work to help people, after all. It was just good to know he was making a difference.

Hearing a knock on the door, Michael raised his eyes then quickly put them back to his watch as he counted Mr. Gurman's pulse. A nurse stuck her head in.

"Dr. Sanford, I have a question," she began.

Michael finished with the pulse and nodded at the patient—everything checked out just fine. He picked up the chart to note it. "What is it?" he asked the nurse as he pulled a pen from the pocket of his doctor's coat and clicked it on.

"Well, it's a strange one," she said, stepping into the dimly lit room. She leaned against the doorway and crossed her arms. "Can I ask what your blood type is?"

Michael stopped what he was doing and looked over at her. A strange one indeed. "Why do you need to know that?"

The nurse laughed nervously. "Sorry, Doctor. I know it's weird to ask."

Michael just looked at her, waiting for her to go on. Generally he was patient, but when he was working, he liked people just to get to the point. Too much to do, too many people to take care of to spend time beating around the bush.

"Well," the nurse continued, straightening up again, "there's a guy in the ER who needs a transfusion, and he's got a rare type. O negative. The blood bank's low and they're asking for people with that type to donate."

Michael finished writing his note in Mr. Gurman's chart, then clicked his pen and put it back in his pocket. He said goodbye to his patient, promising he'd be back the next day to check on him, then headed toward the door. When he met the nurse, he put a hand on her shoulder and walked with her into the hallway.

"This guy doesn't have any relatives?" he asked, quietly closing the door of the room behind him.

"A few kids and an ex-wife," the nurse replied. "We got in touch with his son and he's on his way. But none of them have his blood type."

Michael looked down the hall. It was busy, as it usually was at the changing of shifts. Nurses caught up with one another at the station, exchanging stories about their personal lives as much as they talked about their patients. Orderlies wheeled patients out for tests and back, on gurneys and in wheelchairs. It was controlled chaos, and Michael used to love it. Before he'd met Carolina, sometimes he would stay nearly all night—after midnight at least. He would see more patients, do more paperwork, join in the chatter in the break room, anything to keep from going home to Julie. He'd gone to great lengths to isolate himself in those days. He wasn't proud of that fact, but at the time he couldn't see any other way.

How things have changed, he thought. These days he couldn't wait to get home. He still gave his patients the best care possible, and he never left the hospital or his office until he'd seen to all the responsibilities on his plate. But as soon as he could get away, he raced home and ran into the arms of the woman he loved. It was the only place he felt safe, and where he was most loved. The only place he wanted to be at the end of the day—today especially. Carolina had told him earlier she'd been feeling some cramps and even had a little bit of bleeding. Nothing to worry about, she'd said, but still Michael did. He worried. Today and every day. How could he not? Carolina and the baby were the world to him.

He turned back to the nurse. "Well, it's that guy's lucky night," he said, reaching into his pocket and taking out his wallet. He took out a blood donor card and showed it to her.

She looked surprised. "You're O negative!"

"That I am," he replied as he put the card and wallet back. "So, what can I do to help?"

"Come with me," she said, grabbing his arm and leading him toward the elevators.

On the way down the ER, the nurse filled him in on the patient's background. A man in his forties, he had been in some sort of car crash, a nasty one with a big truck on the freeway. The guy had been driving, and there'd been some impact to the windshield—that meant head injury, and Michael wasn't surprised to hear the man was in and out of consciousness.

"This is a great thing you're doing, Doctor," the nurse said to him as they hurried down the hall and into the emergency room. Talk about chaos—Michael's floor was an afternoon in church compared to this. Doctors and nurses rushed everywhere, patients yelled out in pain, phlebotomists with their carts hurried from one curtain to the next.

Just as I remember it, Michael thought. It had been years since he'd worked the ER, but, as they say, the more things change, the more they stay the same. It looked just like it did the last night he'd left it.

"So who should I see here?" he asked the nurse.

"Oh, Dr. Weiss," she said. "He should be—yes, there he is." She pointed over toward a computer terminal where a slight man with black, curly hair squinted at the screen.

"Great," Michael said. He put a hand on the nurse's shoulder again. "I can take it from here. Just go back and take good care of my patients."

The nurse thanked him, then headed back to her floor. Michael went over to Dr. Weiss to see what he would have to do here.

"I heard you need some O negative," Michael said by way of introduction, and Dr. Weiss looked up.

"Michael Sanford," he said, thrusting out his hand for a shake. "How long's it been?"

"Too long," Michael said, grasping his old colleague's fingers. "But I'll tell you," he said, looking around, "I don't miss this place."

"I bet you don't," Dr. Weiss said, clapping him on the shoulder. "So, you're really here to donate blood?"

"That I am," Michael said. "What do I have to do?"

"Well, head to the blood bank as soon as you can. Tell them you're there for patient..." He turned back to his computer and drew up a file. "Patient Anderson. I'll give you his case number."

Michael laughed a little. "Anderson? That's funny. That's my—"

He stopped cold. The nurse's description of the patient came back to him. Forties, three children, an ex-wife. Carolina's last name was Anderson.

"What's his first name?" he asked Dr. Weiss.

"Uhh..." Dr. Weiss consulted his file again. "His first name is...David."

Michael grabbed the desk and closed his eyes tightly. *This cannot be happening*, he thought, then opened his eyes and looked all around him again. Everything was bright lights and loud noises, pain and suffering and grief. He had to get out. The air in there was stifling him.

"Do you want to see the guy?" Dr. Weiss asked, standing up from his chair. "Put a face to the name of the person you're going to help?"

Michael took a deep breath and tried to compose himself. "I, uh..." He didn't know what to say or what to do. All he could think about was getting out of there and driving right home; all he wanted was to fall into Carolina's arms.

Carolina, he thought, fumbling for his cell phone. "Just a minute, okay?" he said to Dr. Weiss, who nodded in understanding. Michael turned away and opened up a text message.

Are you okay, babe? he typed quickly, then waited for a response.

After just a moment it came in. *Doing better*, Carolina said. *The cramps have subsided. Feeling good now. I'll feel better when you get home.*

Michael hesitated. What should he tell her? Should he say anything about David being in the ER? *No, I can't tell her that*, he thought. *Not in her condition.* Besides, he couldn't be one hundred percent sure it was David. There could have been more than one man with his name in Seattle.

He turned to Dr. Weiss. "Can I see him now?"

The doctor nodded. "Right this way." He got up and walked to a curtain.

Michael slowly followed, the twenty feet across the floor feeling like a million miles. With each step his heart beat faster and harder; he took some deep breaths to try to calm himself. When he reached the curtain, Dr. Weiss pulled it back slowly. Michael took one last breath, then let it out and stepped inside.

In the bed lay a motionless figure in a hospital gown, hooked up to a dozen tubes and wires. He had a heart monitor, a blood pressure cuff, a couple of IVs. A tube down his throat did the breathing for him; the *shh, shh* of the ventilator was the only sound in the room.

As he took it all in, Michael sighed, not wearily but with sadness. There was no doubt about it: this was David. Carolina's David. Michael had never met him personally, but he'd seen him in Carolina's pictures.

"Thanks," Michael said. "Listen, I'll head right over to the blood bank."

Dr. Weiss shook his hand again. "Thanks, Michael. You're a good man."

Unable to say any more, Michael smiled and nodded, then bowed out of the curtain. He left the ER. In the hallway it was quieter, and he took a moment to catch his breath, a moment to think. He leaned against a wall and considered his options.

Should I give him the blood? Of course this would be the right thing to do. This was David, his true love's ex, the father of her children. Such a situation—well, who would blame him if he didn't want to get involved? He could just leave now, get in his car, go home, and forget this ever happened, pretend that nurse had never found him to ask about his blood type.

But Carolina will find out, he realized. What would she think if she found out Michael knew about David but hadn't told her—that he'd just waited to let her find out from somebody else? She wouldn't like it, he was sure, and he wouldn't be able to live with himself.

"That's not why you became a doctor," he reminded himself. He couldn't just ignore David. He'd taken an oath in med school: *If it is given to me to save a life, all thanks. But it may also be within my power to take a life; this awesome responsibility must be faced with great humbleness and awareness of my own frailty. Above all, I must not play at God.*

"I must not play God," he repeated. It wasn't his job to do that. Nor was it his nature. Michael was a good man, and he could never look away when someone needed his help. No matter who it was. No matter what they'd done. And David—well, he hadn't done anything. All he'd done was had the good fortune to meet Carolina before Michael did. He never hurt her. He deserved a chance to live.

Michael took out his phone again and hit the speed dial for Carolina. It was a long walk to the blood bank. He would call her on the way.

Sixteen

Sometimes, Carolina looks at David and questions herself. Why had she left him? He was such a kind man, a wonderful father to their children, a good companion with so many great qualities. He had loved her deeply—and, as far as she knew, he still did. She would always love him in her own way as well, though not the way she had twenty years ago. The love she experienced now with Michael was on another level, the kind one only finds with a soul mate.

"Can I have some water?" David asked her from the bed, drawing Carolina away from her thoughts. She rose from the sofa by the window and went over to him.

"I thought you were asleep," she said softly, reaching down to touch his cheek. It had been a week since his car accident and he still had a bandage covering most of his forehead. She wanted to check for fever but didn't want to touch his healing wounds and risk putting him in any further pain.

"I was," he replied. He sounded hoarse. Carolina took the glass from his nightstand—*her* nightstand, she thought; that used to be her side of the bed—and went into the bathroom. She turned on the tap and let it run until the water was icy, then filled the glass. Going back to the bedroom, she put it down again and leaned over David.

"C'mon," she said gently, linking her arm in his. "I'll help you sit up."

"No," he immediately protested. "No, it's okay."

"David, let me help you," she insisted, leaning over farther to get a better hold on him.

"Carolina, no! You shouldn't be lifting anything with— I mean in your—" He waved a hand in the direction of her protruding belly.

"Oh," Carolina said, standing up straight and backing away a little. "Oh, well. Thanks." She didn't know what to say. David's looking out for her while she was carrying another man's child was awkward, to say the least. Carolina was surprised that he'd even continued to speak to her after all the hurt she'd caused. Now, he had all this physical pain along with the hurt of losing his wife to another man. Carolina continued to feel an overabundance of guilt.

With a little grunting and straining, David managed to push himself up to a sitting position all by himself, then leaned back against the headboard. Carolina handed him the water glass, then sat down on the edge of the bed. "How's your head feeling?"

David took a long, slow drink and swallowed carefully. Then he put a hand up gingerly to his bandage. He winced a little. "Still tender," he said. "But not as painful as my broken heart."

A tear streamed down Carolina's face. "So do you want to talk about it?" she asked him gently as she took the glass back from him. It was empty—he'd finished it all, and rather quickly. He hadn't had much appetite yet, but Carolina was glad he was hydrating himself.

"About what? The accident?" he asked.

Carolina nodded. She didn't want to push him, but her curiosity got the best of her; she needed to hear the details. The doctors hadn't relayed too much information to her. They'd said David had been unconscious for hours when he was brought into the ER. If he hadn't woken up, if the swelling in his brain hadn't gone down, who knew what might have happened. In all he'd been hospitalized for five days. And when he came home, Carolina was right there to help him. No questions asked—by her or by him.

He was lucky to survive the crash, they'd said. But she just had to know...

"Did you lose control of the car?" she asked.

David looked at her, his eyebrows slowly lowering. He winced again as if this caused him pain. "Obviously I did," he said. "How else would it have happened?" He eased himself to lie down again. "Sorry," he said once he was back under the covers. "I shouldn't snap at you. I know you're just concerned."

"It's okay," Carolina said. "I'm just happy you're still speaking to me." She grabbed his hand as if it were the most natural thing in the world to do. "I don't mean to pry. I just..." She tried to think of the right way to say it. "Well, David... You didn't do this...on purpose, did you? You weren't trying to take your own life, were you?"

There was silence for a moment. Carolina just looked at David. He looked back at her, his expression blank as if he were struggling to understand what she'd said.

"I just mean," she went on, "you know, with all the hurt I've caused you, the way things are between us, and now with the girls coming to live with me, it's a lot to handle—"

"Carolina," David said, squeezing her hand. "Stop, just stop." He sat up a little and leaned back on his elbows, so he could look her right in the eyes. "You think I was trying to *kill* myself? How could you think that? I just wasn't focused. I wasn't paying attention while I was driving. How could I? My life has turned upside down."

Carolina looked back at him, but her gaze faltered. Hearing it out loud like that—okay, maybe her idea was a little extreme. But sitting in the hospital with him, listening to the ventilator pushing air into his lungs, wondering if he would ever get back to the life he knew, her mind had wandered a bit. He'd been so distraught over their breakup, and though he'd agreed to let Lindsay and Alexis live with Carolina, she knew deep down he wished they would stay with him. This was so much change in his life, so much all at once. So what if he had been despondent and he'd found himself on a lonely road with a big curve and a steep drop-off...

"No," she whispered, looking down at the duvet. "I guess I don't really think that. I'm just—" She looked up at him again. "I worry about you. I will always worry about you. Is that stupid?"

David raised a hand and put it on her arm. "It's not stupid. It's actually very sweet. Thank you for still worrying about me. If it weren't for you coming here to take care of me, I wouldn't be doing so well now." David laughed a little, then put a hand up to his bruised ribs, which ached every time he moved. "You and whoever donated blood for me."

Carolina looked up again, feeling a little more at ease. David could have gotten mad at her or told her she was crazy, but he'd taken her question very gracefully. *Same old David*, she thought. *Never got himself riled up about anything.*

"Who donated blood for you?" she asked. She knew he'd had a transfusion while he was in the emergency room—Patrick had told her about that. He'd also said the doctor was asking for any donors in the family. The blood bank was low on David's type, and though they wouldn't deny him what he needed, they asked for people to donate to replenish their supply. Unfortunately Carolina wasn't a match, and neither were any of the children.

David shrugged at her, then gripped his shoulder and rotated it slowly, working out some sort of kink. With each minute that passed, it seemed, something new hurt. "I don't know who it was. The doctor said they were asking the staff around the hospital and came up with someone who was O negative." He stopped and thought for a moment. "I wish I knew who it was. I'd like to thank them personally."

"Hm, yeah, that would be great," Carolina said a little absently, her mind working up to a thought. *O negative*, she repeated silently as she reached over to help David rub his shoulder. There was something about it. She'd forgotten it was David's blood type; in all the commotion since his accident, she guessed, it was just a little detail she hadn't needed to remember. Now that he said it again, though, it sparked something in her memory.

"You should lie down again," she told him. "Do you want to eat yet?"

"Mmm, maybe I could handle some soup," David said as he nestled back under the blanket.

Carolina smiled at him and patted the duvet. "Okay. I'll go heat some up for you. Close your eyes now. See if you can sleep a little 'til it's ready."

With David settled, she left the room, closing the door quietly behind her.

Downstairs, she moved through the rooms of her old house, feeling like a stranger in what once was her home. In the kitchen doorway she paused, a flood of memories washing over her. Homework with the kids, family meetings and meals—she'd loved this room for a reason. She'd had so many good times in there, so many happy moments she would never forget. Just the little things of everyday life, but they meant the world to her.

Being back there again was hard. It reminded her of what she'd left behind. But she had a new reality now—a very good one. She and Michael and *all* of their children would build new happy memories together. She just had to work on that and remember always to look ahead to the future.

In the refrigerator she found a container of soup she'd made the night before for David. She poured a healthy serving into a pot and set it on the stove to warm, then sat down at the island and just enjoyed the peace and quiet of the kitchen. It was only one o'clock—a few more hours yet until the kids would come home from school. Lindsay and Alexis would meet her there, then they would all go home later together.

Home, she thought, and a warmth spread through her body. She loved having the girls living with her, loved hearing them laugh and bicker, loved—despite their protests that they were too old for it—tucking them in at night, loved the relationships they were developing with Michael. He got along with them so well, and they seemed to enjoy being with him as well. In time, Carolina was sure, they would fall in love with him too.

As she got up to stir the soup, her mind wandered back to what David had said about the blood transfusion, then to the night of the accident. She'd been in bed already, not asleep but reading a book. She'd had cramps and spotting throughout the day, and she wanted to rest a bit. Michael had messaged her all evening from the hospital, and then later on, just as she was starting to doze off, he'd called her. It was so unusual—normally they just texted all day—she'd immediately worried. Her sixth sense kicked in, a gut instinct that was usually correct.

"What's wrong, Michael?" she'd said as soon as she'd picked up the call. "Are you okay?"

She'd pictured an accident at the hospital, a problem with a patient, maybe even a run-in with Julie. She had never expected to hear what Michael had said next: "David's in the ER, Carolina. He's been in a car crash. It looks pretty serious."

Her heart had sunk. She was so thankful Michael was alright, but she was immediately panicked about David. She'd jumped out of bed and rushed to the hospital, no questions asked.

How did Michael know, though? she thought now. *How did he know David was in the ER?* Michael had been on his regular rounds that night, checking on his own patients. They were in the general ward. He had no reason to be in the emergency room.

Carolina went to her purse and took out her cell phone.

Hey, babe, she typed, *when you called me about David the night of his accident, how did you know he was in the hospital?*

She sent the message off then returned to the stove, where the soup was boiling. She shut down the flame, took a bowl from the cupboard, and poured the soup into it. She went about setting up a tray for David—the soup, some crackers, a glass of juice—while she waited for Michael to reply.

Finally he did. But he didn't message. He called her. Again her stomach dropped, like it had that night of David's accident.

"Michael," she said when she picked it up. "Is everything okay?"

"Everything's fine," he replied quickly. He knew how she worried about him. "I just wanted to talk to you about this instead of sending you a text message." He paused, as if collecting his thoughts. "Carolina, I knew David was in the ER because a nurse came around asking for people to donate blood for him."

"Okay," Carolina asked. "But how did you know it was him?"

"I donated the blood for him."

"You really did that? You donated blood for David?"

"I did."

"Why didn't you tell me?"

Michael let out a sigh. "I didn't want to put anyone in an uncomfortable position. Not you, not me, not David. I...I didn't want him to feel like he owed me anything." He stopped again for a moment. "Carolina, does he know I donated for him?"

"No," Carolina responded, lowering her voice. David surely couldn't hear her from upstairs, but just in case, she didn't want to share this secret with him inadvertently. "He just told me he wished he knew so he could thank the donor personally."

"Good," Michael said. "That's good. He can't ever know."

"But Michael, this is a good thing you've done. A *very* good thing. Why can't he know about it? He just said he'd like to thank whoever helped him."

"Look at it this way," Michael said, his voice low as well. Carolina pictured him in his office at work, hunkered over his desk with all his paperwork and folders. "I took you from him—"

Carolina laughed. "Michael, it's not like you *stole* me or something. I made the decision to leave David by myself."

"Hear me out," he said patiently. "Just hear me out. You left David for me. Then his daughters came to live with us. Imagine how he must be feeling: hurt, lonely, rejected. He's probably wondering what I have that he doesn't."

Carolina grinned. "Well, I could name a few—"

"Okay, not the point," Michael said. "But with all the emotion he's feeling, to have this one other thing hanging over his head—the fact that I did something that helped to save his life—don't you think that's a little too much for him to handle?"

Carolina thought about it. Michael was probably right. To all appearances, David was handling their breakup the best he could. He even seemed okay with the fact that Lindsay and Alexis had moved out of the house. But she knew him, and she knew deep down inside he was truly hurting. He just kept up a good front.

"Okay," she conceded. "I won't mention anything to him. But Michael?"

"Yeah, babe."

Carolina blinked a couple of times, pushing back the tears that threatened to well in her eyes. "I love you so much. For all you are and all you do. Most men wouldn't have donated the blood under the same circumstances. You could have lied about your blood type, but you didn't. You're an amazing man. This is just one more thing I love about you."

"Pssh," Michael replied, as usual blowing off the well-deserved praise Carolina gave him. "Anyone would have done the same. Any decent person, especially any doctor."

"Well, you're beyond decent in my book. As a doctor, as a man, as a human being. You're the best, Michael. I'm so lucky to have you."

Seventeen

How many meetings had Carolina sat through? In the middle of yet another, she tried to calculate. Three a week at minimum, for the twelve years she'd owned her own business. That was...more than eighteen hundred meetings. No wonder she found it difficult to pay attention anymore.

"What do you think, Carolina?" Her bright-eyed assistant, Janine, shot a look in her direction. It was clear she was just trying to keep Carolina involved, but Carolina had no idea what she was talking about.

She smiled anyway. "Whatever you think," she said. "Just go with it." Then she slunk back into her chair and picked up her cell phone.

Remind me why I wanted to come in to work today? she typed, then sent the message off to Michael. It wasn't that she hated being there—just the opposite, she loved it. Even though she only came in a couple of days a week now as her pregnancy got further along, she still felt at home in her office. Everyone was always happy to see her, and she even enjoyed still meeting with clients. For years this place had been her second home, and in all honesty she'd had a hard time leaving it, even if the separation was just temporary. She would go back to it someday.

Today, though, her heart just wasn't in it. She definitely had pregnancy brain; some people said that was an old wives's tale, but Carolina was sure it was a real thing. Lately she just couldn't concentrate on anything, and she was getting so forgetful. That made everything a hundred times more difficult, especially work. She was thankful for her number-one assistant, Janine.

And on top of all that, those awful cramps had reappeared. She'd started feeling them around the time of David's car accident, and they'd come and gone randomly ever since. Some days she felt great, like she was experiencing the most perfect pregnancy in history. Other days she could barely stand up straight. And when the cramps came, so did the bleeding. Not heavily, but enough to make her worry.

Still, her doctor said she was fine. She went to all her appointments, had all the necessary testing done—and some not so necessary, just to be on the safe side. Ultrasounds, amniocentesis, pelvic exams, blood tests, urine samples...she did it all to ensure her baby was healthy. It was. And Carolina was too—she ate right, kept up with moderate exercise every day, and did everything her doctor and all the pregnancy books told her to do. As far as taking care of herself, she went over and above the call of duty. So why did all this pain continue to haunt her?

Excusing herself from the meeting, Carolina went to her office and lay down on the sofa. Closing her eyes, she ran a palm over her belly. With her other hand, she speed-dialed Michael's number.

"Carolina?" he answered on the second ring. "Are you okay?"

Though she'd been trying hard to keep it together, when she heard his voice, she couldn't hold back any longer. The floodgates opened. Tears streamed from her eyes and she could barely speak between sobs.

"Michael," she managed to get out. "I can't take this pain anymore."

"Carolina, baby," he whispered. "It's okay. Take a deep breath. Tell me what's wrong. Are the cramps getting worse? Are you feeling something new?"

She did as he said and inhaled long and slow. Pursing her lips, she let the breath out a little at a time. Then she did it again. Finally she felt able to speak. "Nothing new," she said, her voice wavering. "Same cramps I've been having. And the bleeding." She sniffled and ran a hand over her cheeks, wiping away her tears. "Michael, I know my OB keeps saying nothing's wrong, but I'm so worried. I'm so worried."

"Okay," Michael said. Though he tried not to sound hesitant—he didn't want to alarm Carolina any more than she already was—he was worried too. These cramps had been going on for too long. "Tell me, does it hurt when you press gently on your stomach?"

Carolina tried it carefully, afraid of causing herself more pain—or, worse, hurting the baby. She touched her belly and pushed on it lightly with her fingertips. She let out a breath. "No," she told him. "No, that doesn't hurt."

"Okay, that's good," he replied. "Do you have a fever?"

She put her hand up to her forehead. "Doesn't feel like it. And I don't feel nauseous, I'm not lightheaded… Nothing else is wrong. But this pain, Michael. These cramps. This shouldn't be happening." She started to tear up again. She shifted on the sofa, turning her face against a pillow. She closed her eyes.

"Michael, I think I'm making it happen. I think this is all my fault." The thought had been floating around her head for days now. She'd kept it to herself because she knew Michael would tell her she was crazy, but it was something she just felt deep down in her bones.

more difficult, especially work. She was thankful for her number-one assistant, Janine.

And on top of all that, those awful cramps had reappeared. She'd started feeling them around the time of David's car accident, and they'd come and gone randomly ever since. Some days she felt great, like she was experiencing the most perfect pregnancy in history. Other days she could barely stand up straight. And when the cramps came, so did the bleeding. Not heavily, but enough to make her worry.

Still, her doctor said she was fine. She went to all her appointments, had all the necessary testing done—and some not so necessary, just to be on the safe side. Ultrasounds, amniocentesis, pelvic exams, blood tests, urine samples…she did it all to ensure her baby was healthy. It was. And Carolina was too—she ate right, kept up with moderate exercise every day, and did everything her doctor and all the pregnancy books told her to do. As far as taking care of herself, she went over and above the call of duty. So why did all this pain continue to haunt her?

Excusing herself from the meeting, Carolina went to her office and lay down on the sofa. Closing her eyes, she ran a palm over her belly. With her other hand, she speed-dialed Michael's number.

"Carolina?" he answered on the second ring. "Are you okay?"

Though she'd been trying hard to keep it together, when she heard his voice, she couldn't hold back any longer. The floodgates opened. Tears streamed from her eyes and she could barely speak between sobs.

"Michael," she managed to get out. "I can't take this pain anymore."

"Carolina, baby," he whispered. "It's okay. Take a deep breath. Tell me what's wrong. Are the cramps getting worse? Are you feeling something new?"

She did as he said and inhaled long and slow. Pursing her lips, she let the breath out a little at a time. Then she did it again. Finally she felt able to speak. "Nothing new," she said, her voice wavering. "Same cramps I've been having. And the bleeding." She sniffled and ran a hand over her cheeks, wiping away her tears. "Michael, I know my OB keeps saying nothing's wrong, but I'm so worried. I'm so worried."

"Okay," Michael said. Though he tried not to sound hesitant—he didn't want to alarm Carolina any more than she already was—he was worried too. These cramps had been going on for too long. "Tell me, does it hurt when you press gently on your stomach?"

Carolina tried it carefully, afraid of causing herself more pain—or, worse, hurting the baby. She touched her belly and pushed on it lightly with her fingertips. She let out a breath. "No," she told him. "No, that doesn't hurt."

"Okay, that's good," he replied. "Do you have a fever?"

She put her hand up to her forehead. "Doesn't feel like it. And I don't feel nauseous, I'm not lightheaded… Nothing else is wrong. But this pain, Michael. These cramps. This shouldn't be happening." She started to tear up again. She shifted on the sofa, turning her face against a pillow. She closed her eyes.

"Michael, I think I'm making it happen. I think this is all my fault." The thought had been floating around her head for days now. She'd kept it to herself because she knew Michael would tell her she was crazy, but it was something she just felt deep down in her bones.

"Whoa, wait a minute," he replied, as she had expected. "What are you talking about? How can you make yourself have cramps? Carolina, you haven't done anything wrong. There's no way any of this pain you're having is your fault."

"But it is," she said, her shoulder shaking as she sobbed. "Michael, I didn't want this baby. I didn't want it from the beginning, remember? Maybe all that time I spent wishing I weren't pregnant, or thinking about ending it...maybe that had an effect somehow. I put a curse on myself, and now I'm paying for it." She moaned as another wave of cramps hit her. "I'm paying, and the baby is too."

"Sweetheart, don't think that for a minute," Michael said, and his voice was so low and gentle. Carolina savored it, felt it wrapping around her tired body like a warm blanket. She'd felt so nervous about saying her fears out loud, but Michael's reaction reassured her. She should have known he would. She could talk to him about absolutely anything.

"You didn't cause this," he told her again. "*None* of the pain you're having is your fault. Maybe you had some doubts in the beginning, but that's understandable. Things were so up in the air then. We'd just gotten back from our trip... We didn't know if or when we could be together forever... We just had no idea where fate would take us. Then finding out you were pregnant—that was an enormous surprise. It was all overwhelming, Carolina. You did nothing wrong. You reacted honestly, just like you always do. You were scared, and that was okay."

"It was?" she asked, her voice small and still afraid. She closed her eyes and nestled further into the sofa. "You don't think it's some sort of payback?"

"No," he replied immediately and firmly. "Definitely not. Carolina, you are an amazing woman. The most amazing woman I've ever met. You're smart, and beautiful, and most of all strong. I know that even when you have doubts, even in those rare moments when you're not feeling sure of yourself, you would never do anything to hurt someone else. Especially not our baby. And there's no way your indecision six months ago has anything to do with the pain you're feeling now."

Carolina took a deep breath again and exhaled it slowly. "Alright," she finally agreed. "Alright, I'll take your word for it." She opened her eyes and turned back toward the windows. The sky was gray outside, and she wished for just a little sun. How much good it would do her to see some blue sky just for a while.

"Good," Michael agreed. "Now, let's talk about the pain again."

Feeling a little calmer now, Carolina was able to tell Michael more about how she was feeling—how often she had the cramps, how bad they felt, if she felt anything she thought was a contraction. She'd told him all this before, but she didn't mind repeating it; she was happy to let the doctor take over and tell her what she should do.

"Michael, are you worried?" she asked in the middle of the conversation. He was always so strong for her, always there when she needed him, and he never, ever showed he was scared. Carolina loved that about him; his strength was one of the many, many things that made her feel such an intense bond with him. But lately, she could see it in his eyes: this pain she had alarmed him. He was a damn good doctor, and he knew when something wasn't right with one of his patients. How could he not see it in the love of his life?

"Of course I'm worried, babe," he replied. "I worry about you and the baby morning and night. You two are my world. I only want the best for you. And if either of you is hurting, then I'm hurting too. But we'll get through this.

Don't you worry about it too. That's my job. I'll take care of you."

"Michael," she whispered, tearing up again as another cramp shot across her abdomen. "Michael, I can't take this anymore."

On the other end of the line, there was silence—the sort, Carolina knew, that meant Michael was thinking of what to do. She let him be, as she tried to compose herself, wiping away her tears and sitting up slowly. "I'm sorry," she said wearily. "I'm just so tired. I'm tired of hurting. I'm tired of worrying. This isn't how pregnancy is supposed to be."

"You're right," Michael said, his voice decisive now. "You're right, Carolina. It shouldn't be this way. And we're going to do something about it."

"Michael? What are you talking about?"

"Stay where you are. Lie down, put your feet up, and just wait. I'll be there as soon as I can. I'm going to take you to the hospital, and we're going to get to the bottom of this."

Eighteen

"How about…Jonathan?" Michael asked.

On an examination table in the emergency room, Carolina pursed her lips and let out a long, slow breath as a cramp shot through her abdomen. *Breathe*, she told herself silently, running her palm along her midsection as if that would stop the pain. *In and out, nice and slow. Just breathe and you'll get through this.*

"Jonathan," he repeated. "Ironically that name just came to mind."

When the cramp had passed, Carolina turned her face toward Michael. She tried to smile at him. He was trying so hard, doing his best to get her mind off the pain by running through endless lists of names for the baby. He'd started with A names when they'd first gotten into the room. How long had they been there that he was almost at K?

"I like it. You know, there's something about that name…Jonathan," she replied, her voice low and hoarse, her eyebrows lowered dramatically.

Michael, seeing how uncomfortable she was, grabbed her hand and kissed it gently, then pressed it against his forehead. He closed his eyes.

Carolina let out another long breath, then brought her other hand up to run along Michael's cheek. For a moment she just gazed at him, at the weariness on his face. He was so tired, so worried. She wished she could comfort him the way he was comforting her. But what could she tell him? These cramps, the bleeding, they worried her too. She had no more idea of what was happening than he did, and it seemed like no one at the hospital had much of a clue either. They'd been there for hours. She'd given blood and urine; they'd hooked her up to monitors for both herself and the baby. She'd undergone another pelvic exam. In the end all they could do was wait and see, and every minute that ticked by felt like an eternity.

"How about for a girl?" she asked, trying to shift her weight a little in the bed. She'd been there so long, her hip was starting to hurt. She rolled toward Michael, and with her movement the band strapped across her belly—the one monitoring the baby—slipped a little and for a moment, they lost its heartbeat.

Michael jumped up and reached under her hospital gown. Staring intently at the screen showing the waves of the sonogram, he moved the belt around until it found their little one again. Slowly the *thwup-thwup-thwup* of the baby's heartbeat came back, and they both breathed a huge sigh of relief.

Michael sat down again by Carolina's bedside. He looked in her eyes and she looked into his, and both let themselves get lost for a moment in that old, familiar feeling. The magnetism between them, the push and pull that drew them to one another, was a comfort to them—an old friend who never left their side. When all else failed around them, when everything in the world seemed to be going wrong, they would still have this bond, this electricity. It sustained them; it kept them going. And at a time like this, they needed it the most.

"Jaclynn for a girl," Michael whispered to her, smiling just a little, but warily, sadly.

Carolina smiled too. "It's a good name," she said. "Jaclynn."

On the other side of the bed, the curtain rustled, drawing their attention reluctantly away from each other. Carolina turned her head to see the ER obstetrician coming in, carrying her chart.

"Ms. Anderson, how are you feeling?" the doctor asked, then looked up from the chart. She saw Michael and smiled. "Oh, Dr. Sanford. I didn't realize."

Michael stood up and extended his hand, which the OB shook. "Doctor," he said, and Carolina had to smile a little at his formality. She always found it amusing when she saw him in a work situation. He was so easygoing and laid-back at home, so funny and casual, she was always surprised by how businesslike he was when dealing with patients—or, apparently, other doctors. Carolina admired this about him, though, just one of the many things. She loved how seriously he took his work. He knew he had other people's lives in his hands.

"Carolina is my—" he began to say to the OB, then looked down at Carolina in the bed. "Well, she's my soul mate. The baby is mine."

The OB held a hand up at him. "No need to explain," she said to him with no trace of malice or condescension in her voice. This relieved Carolina. She often found herself at a loss for what to call Michael as well—*boyfriend* wasn't right, not at their ages; *significant other* didn't seem to cover it; *soul mate* it was. But she felt his unease when he tried to explain what he was to her and what exactly he was doing there in the ER.

"Let's get a look at how the baby's doing," the woman said, heading over to the ultrasound machine. Carolina shifted onto her back again, and Michael sat down, quickly grabbing up her hand. They watched the doctor expectantly as she flipped some switches and shot some gel onto the ultrasound wand. She motioned for Carolina to lift her hospital gown, then placed the wand on her belly, moving the strap that was already there to the side for a moment.

The heartbeat faded away again, leaving the room quiet. Outside the curtain all the noises of the ER continued—patients moaning, nurses calling to one another, machines beeping. Everything full of life while in their own little world, Michael and Carolina waited to hear the fate of their child's. Though neither of them had said it—not now, not ever—they were both afraid of what the cramps and bleeding might mean. It could have been a sign that Carolina's body was rejecting the baby.

Perhaps it was only a matter of time until it succeeded.

"Well, there's the baby's head," the OB said as she pressed the wand into Carolina's belly, drawing their attention to the screen. She hit a few buttons on the machine, taking measurements here and there and along the baby's body. Finally she showed them the heartbeat, the one they'd been listening to while they'd sat there wondering what would happen. Carolina and Michael stared at it, the tiny, flip-flap motion of their baby's thumping heart. They heard the sound again. *Thwup-thwup-thwup.* Strong as ever.

"So, what's the prognosis?" Michael asked the other doctor as he gripped Carolina's hand as tight as he could. She squeezed back and closed her eyes, bracing herself to hear the worst.

Whatever happens, Carolina told herself, *it was meant to be, just as everything else that's occurred in our life. I have Michael. He will always support me. However this turns out, I will never be alone.*

"Well," the OB said as she gazed at the screen some more, watching as the baby squirmed.

Carolina opened her eyes. She pushed herself up on her elbows. "What is it, Doctor?" she asked, looking up at the screen as well. Something in the woman's voice alarmed her. Why wouldn't she just come out and say it?

The OB turned to her and smiled. "Everything looks fine," she said, her voice calm and reassuring. "Don't worry. Lie back down," she told Carolina, pushing gently on her shoulder.

"What do you mean everything looks fine?" she asked as the doctor continued probing her with the ultrasound. "That's it? What about the excessive cramps and the bleeding?"

The doctor looked at her again, then at Michael. She shrugged her shoulders. "I can't tell you what's causing those," she said, "but I can tell you there seems to be nothing wrong with your baby. The ultrasound checked out fine, the monitor didn't register any contractions, your blood and urine were good, your cervix isn't dilated…" She moved back from the monitor to give the two parents a clearer view of it. She motioned to the baby's image. "See for yourself. Moving, kicking, turning—everything a baby at this gestation should be doing." She almost laughed a little. "If anything, I'd predict the pain you're feeling is from all the movement. That's quite an active baby you've got there."

Carolina looked at Michael, her eyes pleading with him to tell her it was true. "It is, babe," he said to her, and he almost laughed too, simply from the joy the doctor's news brought him. He rubbed at his teary eyes. "Everything's okay." He looked at the OB. "Right? It's all okay now?"

"Absolutely," the doctor reassured them both as she returned the ultrasound wand to its holder. She sat back on a nearby stool and crossed her arms, the pose doctors always seem to take on when they're explaining something. "Listen,

I know it's scary. Whether it's your first baby or your tenth, it never gets easier. The important thing is you're healthy, your little one is healthy, and I'm sure everything will be fine." She shrugged again. "I'm sorry you're experiencing the cramps and bleeding, but as long as your regular OB is aware of the situation, I wouldn't give either of them too much more thought."

Carolina let out a slow breath again, this time not from stress but from a very profound feeling of relief. "Thank you," she said, reaching out for the OB's hand and squeezing it. She looked at Michael then. "Are you okay?"

He leaned over and kissed her, hard and rough, not caring now what the other doctor thought their relationship was. They were in love—deeply in love, more than anyone could understand. "Carolina," he said, a thought just occurring to him. "I love you so much. Thank God for this. Thank God our baby's okay." He kissed her again, then looked into her eyes once more. "Carolina, let's find out."

She looked at him, searching his face for some explanation. Then it dawned on her. She smiled. "Are you sure?" she asked.

Michael nodded at her, his eyes sparkling and alive.

Carolina turned to the doctor, who'd been watching their exchange with some confusion. "Can you tell us?" Carolina asked her. "We want to know the sex of our baby."

The doctor clapped her hands together, a big smile spreading across her face. "I'd be happy to!" she exclaimed as she stood up and grabbed the wand again, loaded it with gel, and put it on Carolina's belly. A wave here, a press there, and the baby was back again, eyes wide open, staring directly at Michael and Carolina, as if sending them a message.

"Okay," the doctor said, drawing the word out as she leaned in toward the monitor. "Let's see what we've got here." A few moments of poking and prodding, and finally she had what she wanted: a view of the baby's gender.

She turned to the couple. "Can you see it?"

Both Carolina and Michael squinted at the screen.

"Looks like…" Michael began, then he looked at Carolina.

"A…a girl?" she finished for him, completing his thought. They both looked back to the doctor.

"Yes, it's a girl!" she practically shouted. "Sorry, I don't get to tell parents the sex of their baby too often anymore. It's pretty exciting!"

But Carolina and Michael didn't hear her. They were focused on each other. The rest of the world—the doctor, the ER and all its noises—cancelled out by one word: *girl*. It rang through both their minds.

"We have a daughter," Michael whispered to Carolina, leaning over to kiss her once again. "What do you think about that?"

Now it was Carolina's turn to dry her eyes. "I think it's perfect," she said, wrapping her arms around Michael's neck, not letting him go. "I don't know why, Michael, but I just had a feeling." She sniffled and buried her face in his hair. "I had a feeling it's a girl." She laughed then, loud and joyous, happier than she'd felt in many, many days. Finally things seemed to be going right.

Part Three

Nineteen

Carolina and Michael named their daughter Eliza. No rhyme or reason to the name, it just popped into their heads one day and seemed to fit.

"Eliza," Michael had said one morning upon waking. Still half asleep, he wasn't even sure he'd said it out loud.

Carolina rolled over to face him. "What did you just say?"

He looked at her, trying to figure it out himself. "Eliza. For the baby. Isn't it the perfect name?"

Carolina laughed once. "Michael, how'd you come up with that?"

He rolled back and looked up at the ceiling, trying to remember. "I have no idea," he finally admitted. "It just came to me." He looked at her and smiled. "Maybe in a dream."

Carolina put a hand to his face. "Well, ironically, I was thinking the exact same name," she told him softly. "And mine *was* in a dream. Of a beautiful young woman with sandy-blond hair and green eyes, who loved the water and searched for her true love."

Michael gazed deeply into her eyes. "So I guess it's meant to be then. Like you and me... Like our daughter... It's fate, Carolina."

And so it was. Three days before her due date, Carolina went into labor and after only a few short hours, their dear Eliza was born. When Carolina held the little girl on her chest, warm, wet, and crying, she felt a sense of wholeness she'd never experienced before. With Michael at her side and their new love, Eliza, in her arms, Carolina knew her life was now complete. She wanted nothing, she needed nothing. This was exactly where she was supposed to be— the way it was destined to be.

From the very beginning, Eliza was an easy, passive baby, a happy baby—didn't cry much and smiled like it was all she knew how to do. She clung to her daddy and laughed with her mommy, and the bond between the three of them was obvious. Life in the Anderson and Sanford household was beyond good, to say the least—it was amazing. Just how Carolina had known it could be. All those doubts she'd had in the early days as to whether the grass was really greener on the other side, about keeping the baby, about leaving David and starting her new life with Michael—all fell away in time, leaving only a shiny brightness that filled her days with joy and her nights with serenity and peace.

As Eliza grew, she was the perfect fit, that missing puzzle piece in the family. Lindsay and Alexis were always there, acting as little mothers, watching over her, glued to her side. They would guide her, play with her, and give her big-sister advice. Whenever Patrick came to visit, he doted on her; whatever feelings he'd ever had about his parents' breakup seemed to be forgotten. He loved Eliza and he protected her fiercely, like only an older brother could.

Michael's children, Emily and Josh, weren't around much in the beginning. Julie had forbid them from seeing Michael for so long, and after Eliza was born her hatred toward him became even worse. The longer he was away from Julie, the more Michael could see how jealousy ate her up inside and just how that had been a big part of the problem all along. Michael had loved her long ago, but he'd dedicated a big part of his life to other people: his patients. He took his profession very seriously, and Julie had never accepted that. She hadn't wanted to share him. And in the end it had driven him away.

When their divorce was finalized, Julie ended up with almost all the assets—the house, the car, even custody of the children. Michael had conceded it all. It wasn't worth the fight. He'd just wanted an end. Giving Julie whatever she wanted seemed like the only way to avoid an argument. He no longer cared about the material things; he had everything he needed...except his children. He'd hoped for at least partial custody, but Julie would not budge on the issue. However, Michael knew in his heart it would just be a matter of time until his children appeared back in his life.

Though Julie refused to let her children see their father physically, the verbal contact never ceased. Michael spoke to his children nearly every day on the phone. After Eliza was born, Josh and Emily were ecstatic. They both wanted so badly to become a part of her life. They longed to be able to hold her and develop a relationship with their new sister. This brought Michael to tears—not only because of the mere fact that he missed Emily and Josh terribly, but because he was so proud of his children. Occasionally he doubted his role as a father, but, in moments like these, he realized he truly was a good dad. His children had become the young adults he had only dreamed of, far beyond his expectations. They truly *cared* about life, happiness, and, most importantly, others. And that was more than he ever could have asked for.

By the time Eliza began walking, Josh had graduated from high school and headed off to college. He stayed close to Seattle; he loved dorm life and the freedom the experience brought him. He especially loved that his mother could no longer observe his every move—and he was free to see his father as he chose. His visits at Michael and Carolina's house became a weekly ritual, and he built a bond with Eliza that only continued to grow.

At the same time, Emily was feeling more and more pressure from her mother. Without Josh around, it seemed Julie's anger only escalated, and she focused all her controlling tendencies on Emily. She once again forbade her to speak to her father. Emily, motivated and supported by her older brother, rose up against her mother.

"Mom, he's my father," she told Julie one afternoon when she'd caught Emily talking on her cell phone to Michael. "And I love him. And I love his new family. And if I want to talk to him or see him, I will!"

Shocked by her daughter's sudden defiance, Julie hadn't said another word about it...or about anything else. For a long time she gave Emily the same cold shoulder she gave Michael. It hurt Emily deeply, but it also gave her the freedom she needed. Without argument from Julie, she began joining her brother on his weekly visits to their father's house, and finally Michael's family was complete. All his children—including Carolina's—together at last.

* * *

Before Michael and Carolina knew it, they were enrolling Eliza in kindergarten. A beautiful little girl of five with a combination of both her parent's looks and her mother's green eyes, Eliza was perfect in every way: smart, extremely outgoing, friendly, happy… They knew she would go far in life. Still, it was hard to see her start school.

"Can you believe it?" Carolina whispered to Michael as they stood at the edge of the courtyard, watching Eliza line up with the other children in her class.

Michael smiled and waved at his daughter, who grinned at them. She was first in line and enjoying it. "I feel like she was born just a few days ago. Where did the years go?"

Michael thought back on all the last half-decade had brought them. Altogether they had four kids in college—Patrick was first, then Josh; Emily and Lindsay started at the same time as well—and Alexis was already looking at schools. Before they knew it, Michael thought, they'd be visiting campuses with Eliza.

Don't rush it, he told himself. *Let's hold on to this time. Just remember to enjoy it.*

And he did enjoy it. He loved every second of every minute of every day he spent with Eliza, and with her mother. As time went on, Michael's love for Carolina—which he'd thought couldn't grow any deeper—only continued. Every day he saw her in a new light. She was no longer just his soul mate, his lover, but the mother of his child and truly the center of his universe. Every day he saw her strength, her kindness renewed a hundredfold. She was beautiful inside and out. Sometimes he would gaze at her from afar and wonder how he'd gotten so lucky to have her in his life.

But it wasn't luck, he would tell himself at those times. *It was fate.* He had no doubt about that. They were destined to be together.

* * *

When Eliza was in the third grade, she began showing an interest in sports. She was always playing outside with her siblings and her friends, running and laughing and jumping. She was an active girl, coordinated and athletic. Michael and Carolina tried to help her discover outlets for all of her energy. They placed her in jazz and ballet classes, gymnastics, even on a girls's soccer team. They bought her a bike, hoping she would love cycling as much as her father did. They took her hiking, on walks, even the occasional short run. She loved all of it, but none seemed to satisfy her completely. There was nothing she could call her favorite. Her parents hoped she would soon develop a sport she had a passion for.

And then, one afternoon, she discovered tennis.

Carolina had an invitation to play with some of the women from her office and brought Eliza along just to watch. As she sat at the side of the court, the little girl was entranced. Watching the ball go back and forth, back and forth, listening to the *pop* as it bounced against the racquets, she was so intrigued and determined to try it for herself. When Carolina's friends left, she ran up to her mother.

"Mommy, can I play?"

Carolina considered it for a moment. She had an extra racquet, but it would be too big for Eliza. Still, the look in her daughter's eyes—she just couldn't say no to that.

"Sure, sweetheart. But let me teach you a few things first."

For the next few hours Eliza learned the backhand swing, serving, the correct stance—all the moves she'd need to use in a real game. Then Carolina served to her, and to Carolina's surprise, Eliza hit the ball on the first try, hard and over the net.

"Looks like you're a natural!" she called to her daughter, laughing but at the same time overly impressed. Tennis seemed to be the sport Eliza would fall in love with.

On their way home from the club, Carolina stopped at a sports store and bought Eliza her own racquet. They both played a couple of times each week. Carolina found the best tennis coach and enrolled Eliza in classes so she could learn from a pro. Eliza took to it like it was what she'd been born to do. She won trophies and tournaments all through her early childhood and into her teens, and in high school she was captain of the tennis team. When she took the team to the state championships, Carolina and Michael were there—as they had been at every match since she'd started playing—to cheer her on. And when she lobbed the winning ball, they couldn't have been more proud of her.

At least, that was what they thought at the time.

Twenty

Eliza had played some pretty competitive games in her tennis career, but this one had topped them all. This was the state championships, and she went up against the top-ranked high school senior players in Washington.

Well, almost the top, she thought with a smirk as she shoved her tennis shoes in her gym bag and slammed her locker. It wasn't like her to be boastful—if her parents had taught her anything, it was to play her best, but be humble about it—but in this case, she felt she had a little right to gloat. She'd worked extremely hard to get to the top, and she'd finally achieved it. For a few minutes, at least, she was going to enjoy being number one.

Outside the locker room, a crowd awaited her: coaches, local reporters, and, of course, her parents, her number-one fans. Their smiles were even bigger than hers was, and as she approached them, they broke through the crowd and ran over to congratulate her.

"Eliza!" her father exclaimed, a familiar tone of pride in his voice. He put an arm around her shoulders as her mother leaned in to kiss her. "You were *stupendous* out there!"

Eliza laughed. "Stupendous, Dad? Really?"

Michael laughed too and playfully yanked on her ponytail. "Well, what do the kids say these days? Awesome? Intense? Whatever it is, you were *it*. You were on fire."

"Thanks, Dad," Eliza said, all joking aside, laying her head for a moment on his shoulder. She'd always loved making her dad proud, ever since she was a little girl. She remembered for a moment the first time she'd rode a two-wheeler; Michael had been there gripping the handlebar and running alongside her, giving her a pep talk: *You can do it now, Eliza, you can do it!* And the moment he'd let go, he'd cheered and clapped as Eliza had sailed off all on her own.

That was the amazing thing about him, and her mom too. They always supported her independence and loved her no matter what.

"So, can we take you out for dinner to celebrate?" Carolina asked, breaking into Eliza's memories.

"Oh," she said. "Oh, I'd love to, Mom, but I'm supposed to meet Chad." She stood up on her tiptoes, craning her neck to see over the crowd. *Where is he?* she wondered, searching for her boyfriend's light-brown hair among the crowd.

"Well, he can come too," Michael offered.

"Of course," Carolina agreed. "Of course, he's always welcome."

"Well," Eliza said, finally spotting Chad across the court. He was looking around for her. She raised her arm into the air to wave him over and he waved back, then began to make his way to where she was.

While she waited for Chad to get through the mob around her, Eliza took a moment to talk to some reporters, answering questions about her season record and her big win. Michael and Carolina stood one on each side of her, smiling widely as pictures were snapped.

"Hey, how about one with the champion's handsome boyfriend?" a voice called out from the crowd; the photographers parted and Chad came strolling through.

"Well, it's about time," Eliza said to him good-naturedly as he came over and kissed her—a little harder and a little longer than she would have liked. Right in front of her parents, too.

"Sorry," he said, gazing at Eliza adoringly. "I couldn't find you with all the paparazzi." He gave her another kiss, this time a peck on the cheek. "My famous girlfriend." He turned to face the photographers and laughed.

"Chad," Carolina said, "will you join us for dinner?"

"*Mom*," Eliza said before she could stop herself. She didn't want to sound cruel, but she was exhausted from the tennis match. The thought of Chad spending the whole night making a big deal over her—because undoubtedly he would—just made her weary. She didn't feel up to it at the moment.

But it was too late. "Sure, that would be great," Chad said, smiling happily at her mom.

"I can't go out like this, though," Eliza cut in, startling everyone around her. Maybe she'd said it a little too loud and insistently. "I mean, I need a shower. Badly."

"No problem," Chad replied. "I can drive you home so you can clean up and change."

"Perfect," Michael agreed. "Then you can meet us at the restaurant."

"Alright, it's settled then." Carolina leaned over to kiss Eliza again. "We'll see you there, sweetheart. Try not to take too long, okay?"

"Sure, Mom," she answered, trying not to let the strain she felt come through in her voice. Her parents just wanted to celebrate with her; they just wanted to do something nice to let her know how much they cared. She didn't want to ruin it for them with her less than cheerful mood.

"We won't take too long," she assured Carolina as she let Chad grab her bag, then she followed him to his car. He opened the door for her and she hopped in, and in minutes they were out on the freeway, headed toward her home. As Chad drove, Eliza put down her window and enjoyed the wind on her skin. She closed her eyes, thinking about a hot shower and a cold drink.

"So what's next for the amazing Eliza Sanford?" Chad asked her, breaking into the silence she was just starting to enjoy. "You think you'll still play in college?"

Eliza opened her eyes reluctantly and brought her attention back inside the car. She stared out the windshield, though, instead of looking at Chad. How many times had they had the college discussion? And did they have to go through it again now, of all moments?

"Of course I will," she said, trying not to sound as irritated as she felt.

"That's great," Chad said, sounding very enthusiastic. "The U of Washington team will be lucky to get you."

"U of Washington," she repeated absently, looking down at her hands in her lap. She and Chad had spoken about going there together, and though Eliza hadn't definitely said she would, she didn't exactly say she wouldn't either. She'd applied to the university mostly because of the pressure Chad put on her. As far as he was concerned, they were madly in love, the perfect couple, destined to be together forever. But for Eliza, their relationship wasn't quite so clear cut. They'd been dating for two years, which in the world of a teenager was eternity. Chad was a great guy—dependable, fun to be with, good-looking, and popular. Eliza loved him…in a way. But in a bigger way she knew he wasn't the one she would marry. Another important life lesson her parents had taught her: everyone had a soul mate somewhere out there. She just knew Chad wasn't hers. She'd known this in her heart for quite some time. She didn't know how to tell him, though, and so she'd simply stagnated in their relationship, hanging on when she knew it wasn't right.

Just like they did, she thought. Her parents had found one another when they were in their forties. After they had already built their lives with other people, established their careers, their families. Her parents were meant to be together—anyone with eyes could see that—but they'd had to give up so much. It was worth it, but it was so hard for them both. Eliza hoped she wouldn't ever have to wait that long or go through as much as they did.

No, that's not my fate, she told herself, trying to make herself believe it. She might have stayed with Chad longer than she should have, but she had already vowed, even if only to herself, not to stick with him for the rest of her life. She had other plans, other goals that did not involve him. She wanted to make something of herself. She wanted to see the world—and she wanted to find that one person who would make her feel complete. Her soul mate. He was out there somewhere, waiting for her.

So, she'd also applied to other schools—and she hadn't told Chad about it. Schools that were far away from Seattle; schools she knew he wouldn't be willing to go to. One was in California, one of the best and most prestigious in the state. She could get a scholarship there—a full ride—just for playing tennis. She'd already sent in her paperwork and even gone for an interview. She thought she'd done well, but she had yet to get an official offer.

"Here we are," Chad said, drawing her back to reality. He'd pulled into the driveway at her house. Eliza opened the door and hopped out, taking her gym bag with her. As she headed up the stairs, Chad was right behind her.

"You can wait in the kitchen," she told him as she unlocked the front door. Before going inside, she grabbed the mail from the box. "Or the den if you want to watch TV." She glanced at the envelopes as they made their way into the foyer. Bills for her parents, something from Lindsay's school, junk mail, junk mail, junk mail...and then, in the middle of it all, one addressed to her. With a return address from Southern California.

"I'll be down in a few minutes," she told Chad absently, already walking toward the stairs. She dropped the mail on the hallway table, saving that one envelope for herself.

Upstairs in her room, she closed the door and dropped her gym bag. She sat down on her bed, holding the envelope gingerly in her hands.

This is your fate, Eliza, she thought, steeling herself for whatever news this piece of mail might bring. *Good or bad, this is what's supposed to happen for you.*

Slipping her finger under the envelope's sealed flap, she ran it along the top, carefully tearing it apart at the seam. Inside was a single sheet of paper, and she slid it out slowly, then unfolded it. At the top was an embossed crest with the school's name printed below.

Dear Ms. Sanford, it began. *We are pleased to inform you—*

Eliza couldn't read anymore. She jumped up from the bed and then right up onto it, dirty sneakers and all. She pounced on her mattress as if it were a trampoline, slapping her hand over her mouth to contain her joyous screams. When her initial energy subsided, she flopped back down on the bed and continued reading.

...that we can offer you a full scholarship for your achievements in tennis. Please call our office at your earliest convenience to set up an appointment to discuss the details of this offer.

"Oh my *God*," she whispered, again putting her fingers over her lips. She reread the letter, then a third time, just to make sure she'd seen it right. Then she put it back in the envelope and slipped it into the drawer of her nightstand. She ran to the bathroom and started the shower; she wanted to get to the restaurant so she could tell her parents the good news.

For the time being, she'd forgotten all about Chad.

Twenty-One

All through dinner, Carolina could perceive there was something wrong with Eliza. She knew her daughter better than anyone else in the world, and when the girl had a problem, Carolina could sense it without her saying a word. There was just a different air about Eliza when she was troubled; she was irritated, unfocused. Normally so kind and gentle, when something weighed on her mind, she just wasn't herself.

But with Chad there, Carolina didn't want to ask about it. Maybe they'd had a fight in the car; maybe he was acting too clingy again. Eliza had confided that in her mother more than once over the years they'd been dating. Chad was in love with Eliza, that much was clear, but sometimes he could be a little possessive. Eliza was a very independent young woman; she needed her freedom, her space. She loved Chad too, she had told Carolina as much, but she also needed some time to herself—to play tennis, to see her friends, and, most importantly, to pursue her own goals. Eliza was nothing if not intent upon building a good future for herself. Carolina was so proud of her for that. She just also hoped that true love would find Eliza in time, that she wouldn't have to wait as long as she and Michael did.

"Don't worry," Michael whispered in her ear, breaking into her thoughts and once again, as always, reading her mind. "Eliza is fine."

Carolina smiled at him, then glanced across the table at the teenagers. Chad was talking a mile a minute, as he had a tendency to do, about everything—from Eliza's great tennis match to college (again!) to his dog and his parents and his grades. Chad was an outgoing boy, that was for sure, but sometimes, Carolina thought, it was difficult to have a conversation with him. He was a chatterbox, so unlike Eliza, who was much more of a thinker. She enjoyed conversations, of course, but she gave more consideration to what she said. She didn't just open her mouth and let whatever was on her mind spill out. When Eliza said something, Carolina knew to listen because it would be important.

And that was why, when Chad finally took a break and got up to use the restroom, and Eliza said she had to talk to her parents about something, Carolina put down her glass of wine and paid attention.

"What is it?" Michael asked, leaning his elbows on the table, a look of concern on his face as well. Eliza had looked uncomfortable all through dinner so far—he'd seen it too. He was just glad she finally had a moment to tell them what was troubling her.

"Well," she began, glancing out a nearby window as she gathered her thoughts. "Mom, Dad, remember that interview I went to for the scholarship?"

"Of course, sweetheart," Carolina replied. "We thought you did well, right?" She looked at Michael for confirmation.

"Yeah," he agreed. "You did great, honey. Did you hear something back from them?"

"I did," Eliza replied, looking across the restaurant toward the bathrooms—checking to make sure Chad wasn't coming back yet. She leaned over the table a bit, closer to her parents, and lowered her voice. "I got it," she said.

Carolina and Michael glanced at one another, and then their faces lit up with surprise. But, taking a cue from their daughter, they were careful not to let too much of it show.

"Are you kidding!" Michael whispered, reaching his hand out across the table to grab Eliza's. "That's amazing! I knew you could do it."

"Me too, sweetheart," Carolina chimed in. "Neither of us doubted it."

"Thanks, Mom, thanks, Dad," Eliza said with a smile, and she was actually blushing. Carolina smiled too at her daughter's incredible humility. This was a great achievement on her part—a full ride thanks to her tennis skills. She'd worked long and hard for it, and she had every right to be proud of herself. Still, she shied away from the spotlight.

"But listen," Eliza went on. "I haven't told Chad yet."

Carolina nodded. "I know you said you wanted to wait to see what happened first."

"But you're going to take it, right?" Michael cut in, his voice sounding just a little bit urgent. He wanted the best for his daughter—he wanted her to do what she wanted, what made her truly happy. That meant playing tennis and going to the college of her choosing, and becoming whatever she wanted to be in life. Sadly, he knew, Chad just did not fit into that picture.

"Yes, I am," Eliza said, sitting up straighter and looking her parents in the eyes. "No doubt about it. I want this scholarship. This is the school I want to go to. I just…" She trailed off for a moment, her eyes absently roaming the dining room as she gathered her thoughts. She looked back at them again. "I feel like it's fate, you know? Like something's drawing me there. I don't know why, but I feel like I really have to do this."

Carolina and Michael looked at one another, knowing smiles spreading across their faces. "We know just what you mean," Carolina told her daughter, though her gaze remained locked on her partner's. Fate had brought them together; fate had brought them Eliza. There hadn't been a move or a moment in their relationship so far that hadn't felt predestined in some sort of way. From the night they'd both shown up at the fundraiser where they'd met, to the miraculous way they'd survived the storm on the boat, to the name they'd chosen for their daughter all those years ago, something, they knew, had guided their life together. Maybe it was God, maybe it was the universe, maybe it was just a force like karma or kismet. Maybe it *was* luck, as Michael sometimes said. But in the end, the only name they could give it was fate. Plain and simple, they were meant to be together. So they understood more than anyone exactly what Eliza was talking about.

Looking back, they saw their daughter smiling at them. "I know you do," she said. Eliza knew all about their story. They'd shared it with her since she was old enough to understand it. And they'd told her what they'd gone through for one simple reason: they wanted her to understand the importance of doing what she felt was right.

"So are you going to tell Chad?" Michael asked, his voice gentler now. "Or are you just going to go off to college and let him figure it out for himself?"

"Dad," Eliza said with a laugh. "Of course I'll tell him. And I guess I'm going to have to do that pretty soon." She paused for a moment, looking at the two of them. Their opinions meant so much to her; she just had to make sure they approved. "So you think I'm doing the right thing? You think I should accept the scholarship and go there?"

Carolina now reached out to grab Eliza's other hand, creating an unending circle between the three of them. "Absolutely," she said. "You have to follow your dreams, Eliza. You have to do what's good for you."

Michael nodded in agreement. "If you don't, you'll regret it for the rest of your life. You'll always be asking yourself 'what if?' and you'll never have an answer."

Out of the corner of her eye, Eliza saw Chad coming back, making his way around the tables full of other patrons. "Thanks, Mom, thanks, Dad," she said quickly, pulling her hands back from theirs. "I knew I could count on you."

"We're always here for you," Carolina whispered.

"Forever," Michael added. "As long as you need us."

* * *

"Oh, I'm not as young as I used to be," Carolina moaned as she tumbled into bed, pulling the duvet up around her and spooning against Michael. It had been a long day—up early to catch up on some work, then Eliza's match in the afternoon. Just the excitement of that had taken almost her last bit of energy. The glass of wine with dinner completely did her in.

Michael rolled over and scooped her up in his strong arms. She ran her hand down them, enjoying the warmth of his skin.

"Maybe," he said, kissing her forehead, then each cheek, then her lips. "But you still look as beautiful as the day I met you."

Carolina laughed. "Plus a few wrinkles…and maybe a pound or two."

Michael shook his head gently as he took her chin in his hand. He tilted her head up so he could look in her eyes. "None of the above," he told her. "You look amazing. Always have, always will. I've never known a woman as gorgeous as you, Carolina."

With a contented sigh, she leaned her cheek against his bare chest. It felt so comforting after a long and exhausting day. "Speaking of amazing," she said, "how about that girl of ours?"

Michael held her close. "Amazing doesn't begin to describe her. She is unbelievable. Though I knew she would get that scholarship."

Carolina looked up at him and smiled. "I knew it too," she said. "How couldn't she? Even before she won the state championship, she was the best there is." They lay in silence for a moment, each lost in their thoughts about their daughter. "But Michael," Carolina finally said, giving voice to something that had been nagging at the back of her mind since they'd left the restaurant, "do you think what we told her was right? About following her dreams?"

"Of course I do," he said immediately, no doubt at all in his voice.

"I mean, as her parents, do you think that's the responsible thing to tell her? What about stability, safety? What if her dream doesn't work out?"

Shifting away from her a bit, Michael moved so he could look Carolina in the eyes. "Babe, what we told Eliza is the best advice in the world. Think about it: What would have happened if you and I had taken the safe route? If we'd had this dream of ours and chosen to ignore it *because we were scared to fail*?"

Carolina thought about it. If they hadn't risked falling in love, she would still be with David—in an unfulfilling marriage held together only for the children. Michael would be with Julie, a woman who clearly did not love him as he deserved to be loved, who did not appreciate him for the wonderful, gentle, strong, and beautiful man that he was. They would not have this happy home they lived in; most importantly, they wouldn't have their beautiful daughter and all the joy she brought to their lives. Carolina couldn't even bear to think about life without Eliza or Michael, not for a second. Without them there *was* no life for her.

She put a hand to his face. "She has to do it," she whispered. "I get it. She has to." Then she kissed Michael. She let her lips linger on his, savoring the feeling the connection between them brought her: not just love or passion but a sense of belonging. Once again, everything was falling into place.

Twenty-Two

Unsure of exactly what to pack to go away to college, Eliza brought it all: clothes, bedding, just about everything she owned—it was a wonder there was anything left in her room at home. Once she got it all into her dorm—with the help of her dad and her two married brothers, who gladly took the time away from their own families to be with their younger sister on this special day—there were boxes piled floor to ceiling.

"How on earth are you going to fit a roommate in here?" Michael asked as he and Patrick set the last of her suitcases down on her unmade bed. Across the room, in the little empty space that was left, stood another bed and a dresser meant for the other occupant.

Eliza laughed. "Maybe I brought a little too much. I'll unpack some now, narrow it down, and send some back with you."

Patrick and Josh glanced at each other sarcastically.

Eliza knew she could count on her brothers to help her out. Though they were both long out of college themselves, they'd been invaluable in helping her get ready for this new experience—telling her what to expect from her classes and other students, which parties to avoid and which clubs to join, everything she could possibly need to know in order to fit in there. This wasn't Seattle anymore; she wasn't at U of Washington with Chad and able to run home whenever she wanted to. This was a very long drive, far enough even to take a plane. Out here she would really be on her own.

"Are you sure you'll be okay?" Carolina asked, moving over toward her daughter, stepping carefully around the piles of belongings around them. She ran her hand through Eliza's long, sandy-blond hair, so like Carolina's was at her age. She knew her daughter could take care of herself; she'd been fiercely independent her whole life and never suffered for it. She knew when to blaze her own trail and when to hang back with the crowd, and could take advantage of both situations. Eliza had a mind for business already, it seemed, though she wasn't sure if that was the direction she wanted to go. In college, she would find herself. Carolina knew that. She just hoped Eliza would be safe along the way.

"I'll be fine, Mom," Eliza replied in the same tone every teenage girl has used with her mom since the beginning of time: exasperated, but appreciative of the care. Eliza loved her mom; they were practically best friends. But she wished Carolina wouldn't worry about her. She'd be good. More than good, she would do *great* here. She could already feel it. Attending this school really was in the cards for her; as she'd told her parents, this was her fate. Now that it was all coming together, now that she was really there, she felt it even more. Her bond with this school—and whatever or whomever she might find there—was stronger than she'd expected.

"Alright," Carolina relented, kissing her daughter and giving her a hug. "We're going to head home. You'll call us tonight? Let us know how everything went on your first day on campus? And make sure you call home every day."

"Yes, of course," she said, then shooed them all out of the room, locking the door behind them and slipping the key into her pocket. She followed her family back out to their car and they said their goodbyes. The rest of them piled in and drove off, her brothers waving out the window as the SUV receded into the distance. And just like that, Eliza was alone.

She smiled a little smile from the middle of the parking lot, where she watched her family drive away. She shed a tear but knew in her heart she'd be alright. She loved her family, the closeness, and the special bond she had with her parents. Originally she hadn't planned on going so far away to college, but she knew she would easily adapt to the new experience. The one thing that excited her most was the thought of independence, and the distance from Chad.

Ugh, Chad, she thought as she started to walk, a sour taste forming in her mouth. Their breakup had not gone well—at least, he hadn't taken it like she'd thought he would. Eliza had sat him down and explained, very gently but rationally, that she had other dreams, other goals in life, and that she and Chad just didn't want the same things anymore. It made sense for her to go somewhere else to study, especially to a school that offered to pay for her entire education.

"How can I pass that up?" she'd asked him. But the question hadn't fazed him.

"You could pass it up for me," he'd said, hanging his head, staring at his lap. "If you loved me." Eliza hadn't expected him to be happy about her news, but he certainly didn't make it easy on either of them.

In the end, though he hadn't liked the idea, Chad had to agree it was in Eliza's best interest to go to California. He'd tried—for about a minute, and to no avail—to convince her he could transfer to the same school, so they could still be together even though she didn't want to stay in Seattle.

"It's not just Seattle," she'd finally had to tell him. "Chad, we do not have a future together. You're a great guy, but we're just not meant to be together."

The words echoed in her head now. Eliza almost regretted them. She liked Chad, even loved him in a way, but she didn't want to hurt him. She just didn't know any other words to use to tell him how she felt.

"It's not your fate to be with him," she told herself now as she continued to walk, past her dorm and down into the quad. It was such a nice day out—warm and sunny, a beautiful California afternoon—and she needed to clear her head. Might as well get to learn the campus at the same time.

On the main lawn, groups of students gathered, greeting each other like old friends. Eliza pictured herself there next fall with all the new people she would meet this year. She'd never had any problem making friends and figured it wouldn't be long until she had her own crowd to hang around with. As soon as classes started and the tennis team began playing, she would get to know some people.

Spying the courts off in the distance, she headed over that way. She'd seen them when she'd come for her scholarship interview and again when she'd come to accept the offer, but she had yet to play on them. Her racquet was packed away somewhere, so she wouldn't get any play time in today, but at least she could go and check out the competition.

To her surprise, there was a lot of it. The six courts were all full, some with singles, some with doubles, boys and girls mixed. Eliza entwined her fingers in the chain-link fence at the south end of the courts and just stood there, watching the players swinging, the balls popping back and forth, back and forth. What was it about this game that entranced her? She'd loved it for so long yet never stopped to think much about it. Something about tennis just felt right to her—like playing it was something she'd been born to do.

She reflected on that for a moment. If she'd been meant to play tennis…and she felt too as if coming to this school had been the next step she was supposed to take in her life…then was it really all part of some big plan? Had all of these things her life conspired to get her here at this place and this time for some larger purpose?

She grinned a little. *You're starting to sound like your parents*, she thought, and her heart ached a little for them. Independence aside, she missed them already, as she knew deep down she would. She even missed hearing them reminisce—*again*—about how they had met, about how fate had brought them together. She always rolled her eyes at their stories because she was their kid and it was what she was supposed to do, but in reality she loved to hear them. There was something so comforting in knowing how truly and deeply her parents loved one another, and about how much they'd given up to be together and to have her. Eliza couldn't imagine her mom and dad with anyone else. Fate truly had brought them together.

And now it had brought her here, to this school, to these tennis courts. But why? Eliza continued to question herself but couldn't think of a reason. *Well*, she figured, *one day at a time*. The reason would come to her eventually. Everything happened for a reason. She just had to be patient and wait.

In the meantime, she had a ton of unpacking to do. Satisfied with the taste she'd gotten of the school's tennis scene, she turned around and began to head back toward her dorm, but when she was only a few steps away from the fence, a fuzzy, yellow ball bounced by, landing just in front of her feet. She stopped short and automatically picked it up. Bouncing it up and down on her palm, she turned back toward the courts.

"Hey, over here," a deep voice called, drawing Eliza's attention back to where she'd just stood. Her eyes fell on a young man with brown, sun-streaked hair and green eyes just like hers. He wore a white tank top and his arms... *Oh*, Eliza thought, *his arms are...perfect.* Finely muscled, they flexed as he raised his hands up over his head and gripped the chain-link with his fingers.

"Sorry," he called to her. "Sometimes I don't know my own strength." He grinned at her, and Eliza felt her knees go weak. "Would you mind tossing it back?"

"S-sure," Eliza stammered, silently cursing her nervousness. She held the ball tightly in her right hand, reared back, and threw it over the fence. It landed well behind the boy...but he didn't turn around for it. Instead he continued to stare at her, that enigmatic smile on his face. Eliza gazed back, finding herself unable to look away.

"Thanks," he finally said.

"Sure," Eliza said again. "Anytime."

"John!" someone called from the other side of the court. "Come on, we've got a game to finish!"

The young man remained still for another moment, then slowly let go of the fence and lowered his arms. "Gotta go," he said to Eliza. "Thanks again." He began to back away slowly.

"You're welcome," she managed to get out this time, standing still and watching him as he went. Finally he turned and jogged back to his friends.

Eliza turned and ran. Back across the quad, all the way to the dorm, not stopping until she stood in front of her door. Once inside, she locked it and—after navigating through her piles of possessions—sat down on her bed. Her heart raced, her mind replaying what had just happened over and over again.

"John," she said. The name sounded so right on her lips. So...familiar. Eliza laughed when she thought this, then she stood up.

"Get your head on straight," she said, reaching for and opening a box. "You have too much to do to get caught up in a crush."

And as she spent the rest of the day unpacking, she kept reminding herself of this. Still, her mind wouldn't let her forget. It kept returning to John—*John*—like an old favorite memory she couldn't quite let go.

Twenty-Three

Eliza was not prepared for dining hall food. She'd grown up on good, home-cooked meals; both her parents were amazing in the kitchen and insisted on sit-down, family dinners most nights of the week. Eliza had spent so many happy hours around the dining room table with Carolina and Michael and her sisters—and her brothers when they could make it.

Now that her only choice was an enormous cafeteria full of people she didn't know, she really began to feel homesick.

But she got her tray of food and headed to a table, determined to make the best of it. *You worked hard to get here*, she reminded herself as she wound her way over to a spot by the windows. *Don't let a little thing like eating alone get you down now.*

Finding an empty seat, Eliza settled in. As she sipped a glass of juice, she sat back in her chair and gazed out the window for a while. What an amazing view—the dining hall was right on the ocean. Nothing but pale sand and rolling waves as far as she could see. Eliza smiled to herself, feeling a warm sensation inside. Just looking at the water, she once again felt like she absolutely belonged here. There was something about the ocean that brought her peace of mind.

"Beautiful, isn't it?" a familiar voice behind her asked. Eliza stopped mid-sip, almost afraid to turn around.

John, she said silently to herself, remembering the name of the young man she'd seen at the tennis courts earlier in the day. Putting down her glass on her tray, she cleared her throat once and slowly, calmly, turned her head his way.

And what she saw nearly took her breath away. Now that he was cleaned up—hair washed, sweaty tank top replaced by a short-sleeve button-down shirt and a pair of loose-fitting jeans—he was even more handsome than she'd realized. She took him in for a minute, trying not to smile too widely.

"The ocean, I mean," he said, grinning back at her playfully. "Mind if I sit here?"

Before Eliza could answer, John set his tray down across from her at the table. He took a seat, never taking his eyes off of her once.

"Sure," Eliza said, laughing a little. "Be my guest."

John laughed too, and Eliza was surprised by the easy rapport between them. They were already so comfortable with one another, almost as if they'd known each other for years.

"And yes, it is beautiful." She turned to look out the window again. Big waves rolled in and crashed on the shore, the pale green water cresting into white foam. "I love the ocean." She looked back at John, squinting as she thought. For some reason she wanted to tell him how drawn she was to the water, how it had actually been a factor in her considering this college. She couldn't explain it, but she just felt like she could pour out her heart to this stranger.

"I love it too," he said, his eyes also out on the water, his voice distant and dreamy. He looked at Eliza, a smile starting to play on his lips. "Are you from around here?"

"No, I grew up in Seattle," she replied. "How about you?"

"Savannah," John said, never breaking away from her gaze.

"Georgia?" Eliza asked, and John nodded in reply. "I've always wanted to go there. I hear it's lovely."

Now John did smile. "It *is* lovely," he said, his eyes wandering over Eliza's face. She felt her cheeks blush to a deep, dark pink.

"How'd you decide to come here then?" she asked, her voice raspy with embarrassment.

John shook his head a bit, as if bringing himself out of a trance. He looked down at his tray full of food, picked up his fork, and started stabbing the broccoli spears on his plate. "I don't know exactly," he said, then took a moment to bite and chew. "I just felt...compelled to be here. Is that weird? That's weird, isn't it?"

Eliza laughed a little. Now she couldn't take her eyes off of him. Who was this boy who loved the water like she did, who played tennis like she did, who felt as if being at this random, faraway school was somehow his fate...just like she did?

"Not weird at all," she replied, digging into her own dinner as well. "In fact, I...I sort of feel the same way."

John grinned at her, a big, comfortable smile. "Get out," he said.

Eliza smiled too. "No, really," she said. "I had other offers, and I sort of had plans to go to U of Washington." An image of Chad flashed through her mind—sour, scowling Chad who never wanted her to do what truly made her happy. She peered at John again, wondering if he could be the same: controlling, unbending, immature. Somehow, she knew he couldn't. He wasn't Chad—he was completely different. She didn't know John well, but somehow she knew he wasn't the type of guy who would ever hold her back from doing what she was truly meant to do.

"That's a good school," John said, glancing out at the ocean again. "But I have to say, I doubt it's got views like this."

Over the course of their meal they continued to talk and talk—Eliza was amazed by how easy it was to open up to John. Though they had just met, she felt like she could tell him anything, and sometimes she did. She talked about her family, and Seattle, and her high school, and even Chad and their awful breakup. John listened attentively, nodding and asking questions and hanging on Eliza's every word like everything she said was the most interesting thing in the world. He told her about Savannah and even said he'd love to take her there one day.

Before they knew it, dinner was over at the dining hall and they were the last two students in the place—it was just them, no one or nothing else seemed to matter. They were completely oblivious to the sound of the ocean and the guy across the room vacuuming the carpet. John stood up first, grabbed Eliza's tray, and ran over to drop it at the kitchen window for her. Then they made their way outside.

Back in the balmy sunshine, Eliza felt suddenly tired. Happy, but tired. All that food and good conversation had worn her out.

"So are you busy tonight?" John asked as they walked toward her dorm, taking Eliza off guard.

"Uh," she began, her mind immediately picturing all those boxes back in her room. "I have a lot of unpacking to do..."

"Oh, come on," John said, then laughed. "That can wait. We're having a bonfire on the beach tonight. Come with me. It'll be a lot fun."

Eliza considered it. "Who's we?"

"Oh, the tennis team. It's sort of a ritual—every first night back on campus we go down to the beach and have a little party." He grinned at her again. "Nothing funny, don't worry. Just a bonfire and some good friends."

Eliza smiled back at him. "Oh, good," she said. "I was wondering when I'd get to meet my new teammates."

John looked at her quizzically for a moment, his mind putting two and two together. "Oh, you're—" he started, then brought up a hand and rubbed his chin. "You're on the tennis team?" He thought again. "Don't tell me you're the state champ I've been hearing so much about."

Eliza did a little bow. "That would be me," she said. "Undefeated for the last two seasons, captain of the team that brought home the title."

John stopped walking and just looked at her. After a moment, Eliza began to blush again.

"What?" she asked him with a nervous laugh. "Why are you looking at me like that?"

John's face grew serious. "Because I can't believe I've ever met a woman so perfect."

Twenty-Four

When do we ever expect to fall in love? No one can answer that question. Love just happens when you least expect it, not when you're looking for it. This emotion sneaks upon us in an instant, this powerful feeling we have no control over. It comes to us unasked for, yet we welcome it with open arms even when we don't quite fully understand it.

Closely watching John in the light of the bonfire, talking and laughing with his friends, Eliza observed every little thing about him. He was so personable; he was absolutely wonderful. She wasn't in love with him—not yet anyway. They'd only just met. But there was something deep inside of her that knew in time she could be. Something about John spoke to her. No, it *called* to her. Like the fate that had brought her to this school now dragged her in his direction.

John felt the same way too, Eliza was sure of it. She could see it in his eyes, sense it in his stare. They couldn't take their eyes off of one another; even when they spoke to other people, they always glanced back, seeking reassurance or simply a thrill. That was what Eliza felt when she looked at John: an electrical impulse, emanating from the depths of her body. She couldn't explain it, not even to herself, but something connected her to him...something, somewhere, sometime.

"Let's go for a walk," he whispered in her ear, then grabbed her hand and led her away from the fire.

"Hey, John, where you going?" someone called after them.

"Yeah, where're you taking our new star player?" another called, and John simply waved a hand at them, a good-natured smile on his face. Eliza had been a hit with the tennis team—they'd all heard about her and couldn't wait to meet her. And Eliza liked them too. She couldn't wait to get to know them better.

But for the moment, there was only one person she wanted to be with.

"So what do you think of the team?" John asked as if reading her thoughts. Tugging on her hand, he led her closer to the water. The remnants of a cool wave ran over her toes, and she shivered.

"They're awesome," she replied, then smiled mischievously. "But we'll see when we get on the court."

John grinned at her in response. "You're pretty competitive, huh?"

"Yeah, I am," Eliza said, not the least bit embarrassed about it. She knew she had talent, and years and years of practice had honed her skill. She never bragged about winning, but she knew she was good. And she was confident enough not to shy away from that.

"That's good." John nodded, looking out over the ocean. "I am too. I was on the rowing team in high school. We made it pretty far—we weren't state champs or anything, but I took it seriously. I liked to win. If I hadn't started playing tennis, I'd probably still be rowing today."

"Rowing?" Eliza asked absently, her eyes wandering out to the horizon as well.

"Yeah." John stopped and looked at her. "Rowing. Why?"

Still holding his hand, Eliza just looked up at him. His green eyes sparkled like the light of the moon dancing across the surface of the water. What *was* it about rowing? Why had she said that? She wasn't sure herself. She just felt a strange connection with it.

"I don't know," she told him, and they resumed walking. "I never rowed in my life." She laughed a little. "I've barely even been on a boat. My parents had this terrible accident during a storm, before I was born... My mom almost drowned. So they've been a little leery of the water ever since."

"Really?" John asked. "I couldn't live without it. I mean, I understand why they feel that way. But I can't imagine never being out there again."

Eliza looked up at him and smiled. He was a year older than she was and a good six inches taller. Big, handsome, strong—Eliza felt so lucky to have met such a good-looking young man. "We should go together sometime, out on a boat."

John stopped again. His grin spread from ear to ear. "Why, Eliza, are you asking me on a date?"

Eliza blushed again, but then she laughed. "Well, yes, I guess I am," she said.

"Then I accept," John said, pulling her in for a quick hug. "Now, all we need to do is find a boat."

Eliza was jolted by John's embrace, shocked by how safe she felt in his arms. She felt so protected, she wanted to stay there forever, locked in time by the edge of the sea.

"You get along with your parents?" John asked, pulling Eliza out of her reverie. He stepped back from her then with a fast squeeze of her shoulder and led her once again down the shore.

"Oh, um, sure. I mean yes. Really well, actually. They're my best friends."

"Wow," John said. "You don't hear many people say that these days."

Eliza shrugged. "Well, it's true. I mean they've always been there for me, always supported me. They've taught me so much, and they've been through so much themselves... They didn't meet until they were in their forties. They were both married with kids already." Eliza laughed a little, a warm feeling growing in her heart. She loved the story about how her parents had met, and this was really the first time she'd gotten to tell it. "They literally saw each other across a crowded room, and something drew them to one another. Some force pulled them together. It might sound silly, but that's the way they describe it. Once they met they just knew they could never be apart."

"It's not silly," John said with a smile. "It's very romantic." He stopped walking and once again pulled Eliza in his arms. He rested his chin on her head. "Do you mind?" he asked.

Eliza nestled into his embrace, pressing her cheek against the soft fabric of his hoodie. "Not at all," she whispered. "I was kind of hoping you'd do this again."

They stood that way for a long time, or at least it seemed so to Eliza. With one ear she listened to his heartbeat; the other tracked the movement of the sea. Beating and crashing, beating and crashing, a rhythm only she could hear, as if it were meant just for her. Pulling her head back, she looked up at John.

"Do you believe in fate?" she asked him, her voice barely a whisper. She looked deeply in his eyes, searching for what she hoped would be the truth: that he felt the same about her as she did about him. That he felt this attraction. That something told him they should never be apart.

"I believe in a lot of things," he replied, his voice soft too, as gentle as the glow of the stars in the sky. "I believe in love. I believe in hope. I believe in fate." He trailed off and let the silence sit between them for a while, the swell and rush of the waves the only sound. "And I do believe in fate, Eliza. I believe that's what brought me here. And I believe it's why we're standing here together tonight."

Twenty-Five

"Man, are you going to see Eliza *again*?"

Looking in his mirror as he buttoned up his shirt, John shot a look at his roommate over his shoulder. "And what's wrong with that?" he asked, trying to sound sarcastic and offended. But then he couldn't help smiling wide, like he did every time he heard her name.

His roommate smiled too. "Nothing," he said, "nothing at all. That's a great girlfriend you've got there. You should consider yourself lucky she gives you the time of day at all."

Finished with his shirt, John ran a hand through his hair, then turned to his dresser. Keys, wallet, all the essentials. He stuffed them in his backpack. "Oh, I do," he said to his roommate as he zipped up the bag and hoisted it onto his shoulder. He turned to his friend. "I'm the luckiest guy in the world. Don't wait up, okay?"

And with that, he left. He hurried down the hallway, full of loud and raucous students as usual. Another Friday night on campus, nothing out of the ordinary. Everyone was getting ready to go out—to parties, to the bars, wherever was cool these days. John had other plans, though, and he laughed to himself as he navigated through the crowd.

If only they knew where I'm headed, he thought, making his way toward the lobby and the doors.

Outside the sun was setting as a cool California evening settled in. John had come to love the weather here—always mild, never overbearing, definitely not as hot and humid as it could get back in Savannah. He hadn't been back there yet this semester; he'd had plenty of chances to return for a few days here and there, but he didn't want to leave Eliza. They spent every minute together that they could. They ate meals together, studied together, and of course went to tennis practice together. They were a true team, inseparable though they'd only known each other a few months.

It's felt like years, though, John reminded himself as he made his way across the quad, approaching the tennis courts. Thinking back, he remembered the first time he'd seen Eliza there, when she'd returned the ball he'd shot right over the fence. There'd been something about her even then, some sort of magnetic pull that drew him to her—and kept him there. From the first time he'd laid eyes on her he'd known he had to get to know her. More than that, he had to make her a part of his life. Little did he know she was feeling the same way. When she confessed it later, he almost couldn't believe it was true.

And now they were inseparable. John only left her side to sleep and go to classes, and at this point he couldn't imagine being away from her for a whole weekend, long enough to return home and visit his family. Maybe in the future—maybe sometime soon—he would make the trip there, and bring Eliza along to meet his parents. They would love her, he was sure, just as much as he did. Who couldn't love a woman as amazing as Eliza?

Outside the library—his exciting Friday night destination—John paused to send a text to Eliza, to find out where she was waiting for him inside. This place was like a second home to her; she spent even more time among the stacks than she did visiting John at his dorm. But that was okay with him. He knew Eliza took her studies very seriously. And he admired that so much. It made him happy to have a girlfriend who was beautiful, talented, *and* intelligent.

Third floor, came her reply. *Table in the back. I saved you a seat. XOXO.*

John hurried into the building and then upstairs, taking the steps two at a time. As usual he couldn't get to Eliza fast enough. Across the huge but almost entirely empty room—he thought of his dorm again, of all those people getting ready to go out partying—he saw her sitting there, hunched over a massive textbook, her hair pulled back in a ponytail. He made his way over as quietly as possible and walked up to her from behind.

"Excuse me, miss?" he said, dropping his voice to disguise it. "I seem to be lost. Could you direct me to the books on stringing tennis racquets?"

Eliza smiled before she even turned to face him. Silly voice or not, she would know her boyfriend anywhere. She dropped her pen on the table and stood up as she spun around, then threw her arms around his neck and kissed him.

"Is that your new major?" she asked him, laughing as he playfully tugged at her ponytail. "Or are you just thinking of taking it up as a hobby?"

"Who has time for hobbies?" he asked as he tossed his backpack onto the table and headed to the other side. As he sat down in an old, creaky chair, the sound of its complaints filled the room. He looked around, expecting a librarian to shush him, but aside from a student or two, he and Eliza were pretty much alone.

He turned back to her. "How's the paper going?" he asked.

Eliza sighed and looked at her notes. "Well, it's slow. Lots of research to do, but once I'm done with all that, the writing should be a breeze."

"Good," said John, reaching for his book bag. He opened it up and pulled out a book and notepad for himself. "Then maybe you can do mine for me, too."

He smiled at Eliza, that winning, amazing grin she couldn't get enough of. She smiled back, unable to contain the love she felt for him…and the desire. John was good-looking, no doubt about that. Often Eliza couldn't concentrate on her studies when he was around. But there was more to him than his looks—so much more. And Eliza had known it from the start. From their first interaction by the tennis courts, she could just sense it about him: he was always a gentleman, an honorable man, with a heart of gold and true to his word. His muscular build was perfect to Eliza, and his face a pleasure to look at. She loved the way his eyes lit up when he saw her and his messy hair after they played a hard match of tennis. But there was nothing she loved more about John than his heart. He was good, and he was good to her. And that was what mattered more than anything.

"Do you really need help with it?" she asked, hoping he hadn't noticed her diversion into daydreaming.

"Nah," he replied, flipping through his book. "I got it under control. Thanks to you and all these study dates you make me come to."

Eliza smiled again and went back to her notes as they continued to chat. They talked about their classes that day, their friends, their upcoming tennis match—anything and everything, as they always did. And as usual they laughed often, sometimes loudly. They couldn't help it. They always had a good time together.

At least they did until the librarian came in to watch them. She didn't tell them to be quiet in so many words, but they could see her glaring at them from the desk across the room. Giggling to themselves, Eliza and John looked around the tables, wondering who, out of the few students there, had turned them in.

"These people are no fun," John said with a mischievous smile. Eliza simply put her fingers to her lips, then went back to reading her textbook.

But now that he was riled up, it was difficult for John to stay focused. He tried to read his book too; he tried taking notes, but nothing was making sense. Not with Eliza sitting across from him. She was too pretty, too tempting. He couldn't take his eyes off of her. But he couldn't talk to her, either. So he thought of something else.

My dearest Eliza, he wrote on an empty sheet of notebook paper. *You mean so much to me. In the short time we've known each other, you've become my world. I can't imagine my life without you in it. Just the thought of you makes me smile like I've never smiled before. I'd give you anything and everything to keep you by my side.*

After reading it over once, he slid the paper discreetly across the table to his girlfriend. She looked at him for a moment, a smile playing on her lips.

"What's that?" she mouthed to him, and he gestured to the paper, urging her to take it and read it. She did, holding it out in front of her so he couldn't see her face. Then she lowered it. She had tears in her eyes. John reached out and touched her cheek.

"Don't cry," he whispered. "Don't cry, Eliza." He pointed to the paper again. "Just write back to me."

Setting the page down on the table, Eliza picked up her pen, chewing on the end of it for a moment as she thought. She set to writing quickly, and in moments she was finished with her reply to him. She picked the paper up and handed it over with a flourish.

Dear John, it began. *When I was a young girl I always dreamed I would meet my own Prince Charming. He would ride in on his white horse and sweep me off my feet, and take me away to live happily ever after. You might not have a horse, but you are that prince to me. I knew from the moment I met you how special you are, and I'm grateful every day to have you in my life. I love you so much. I feel as if I've known you forever, like our being together is meant to be.*

Now it was his turn to well up. But he let the tears go, and he turned to a new sheet of paper.

Eliza, he wrote, *we are meant to be together. Everything happens for a reason, isn't that what they say? Well, you and I happened. Our love happened. There's no doubt in my mind that fate has brought us together—and will never tear us apart.*

When Eliza read this one, a sob caught in her throat. *Everything happens for a reason,* she read again, that phrase echoing round and round in her mind. How many times had she heard those words? All her life, it was what her parents had told her. Things happened for reasons, people appear in your life out of nowhere, without warning and when you least expect it. Eliza had always thought it was a nice idea, and she knew how much her parents believed in it. But until she had experienced it for herself—until she had met John and learned what fate truly was—she hadn't quite believed it.

Now she did. And there was no way she could ever believe otherwise.

Twenty-Six

Every parent wishes for nothing less than pure happiness for their children. Not just being happy but fulfilled. They want their sons and daughters to know joy in their lives without ever having to feel heartache; they want their dreams to come true without the struggle it often takes to get there. They want their daughters to find love without compromise, their sons to be good men, gentle, honest, and kind-hearted.

As Eliza's father, Michael wished for all of this and more. He wanted this kind of man for her, the kind who would appreciate her for the magnificent young woman she was. Chad had never done that; he was a nice boy, but that had been the problem—he was a boy, not yet ready to grow up and certainly not as mature as Eliza was even at sixteen. Sometimes Michael and Carolina joked that their daughter had been an adult since she was two. She'd always taken charge of things, whether it was divvying up the toys at play dates or bossing around her older brothers. She'd had a mind beyond her years for as long as Michael could remember. She was smart and she knew it, but she also knew how to use it.

That was why, when Eliza went off to college, Michael knew she would succeed. She was balanced, well-rounded. She would do well in her classes, on the tennis team, in her social life. Of course he worried, as all parents do, about sending his little girl out into the big world. But even more than that, he trusted her. He knew she could take care of herself and she would always make the right choices, the ones that would benefit her the most. She'd shown him that the day she'd decided to forge her own path rather than following her high school boyfriend around. When she came to a fork in the road, she followed her heart. And Michael could not have been prouder.

Still, when she called from school and said she wanted to bring a young man home to meet him and Carolina, his heart had skipped a little. It was only the end of the first semester, the first winter break. The boy's name was John, she'd said, and he could come spend some time in Seattle before heading to his parents' home in Savannah. Of course Michael had agreed to it with as much enthusiasm as he could muster. But later he confided in Carolina that it scared him.

"Don't you think she's rushing into it?" he'd asked as they'd lay in bed, curled around one another. "She's only been at school a few months. How can she be so serious about anyone yet?"

Carolina thought for a moment before responding. "You know our daughter," she said at last, her voice calm and reassuring. "She's not going to sacrifice herself for the sake of a relationship. If this John means something to her—enough to bring him here to meet us—then there's got to be something special about him."

Michael had to agree with her. Eliza was young but she was far from naïve. He guessed he would just have to trust her—and try not to judge John before he'd even met him.

* * *

"Mom? Dad?" Eliza's voice rang out from the front hallway as a cool breeze blew through the open door. From the top of the stairs, Michael felt it as he saw her coming into the house, a suitcase and a tall young man in tow.

So this is John, he thought, taking a moment before answering to check him out. He was dressed well, neat and casual; his light-brown hair was blown by the wind. As he closed the door behind him, Eliza turned back to him, and the smile he beamed at her was unabashed and real. Michael was taken aback. He knew that look; he knew the feeling behind that look. He'd gazed at Carolina just like that a million times before.

"Hello?" Eliza called again, and Michael knew he had to come out of hiding. Stepping onto the stairs, he took a deep breath, readying himself to meet this man his daughter had brought home. After all he'd been through in his life, this was possibly the most nerve-racking moment he'd ever experienced.

"Hello, hello," he said as he made his way downstairs toward them. Before he even hit the hallway floor, Eliza was running toward him, arms opened wide. She met him at the foot of the stairs, where she practically jumped up into his arms.

"Daddy!" she screamed, and Michael wrapped his arms around her tight.

"Hey, my baby," he said. "I missed you!"

"I missed you too," she said, peeling herself away from him. She stepped back then, holding a hand out to the young man behind her. "Dad, this is John," she said, her voice sounding just the slightest bit unsure—a tone Michael didn't think he'd ever heard from her before.

She's nervous, he thought to himself, and though he wanted to laugh, he managed to keep it to himself. Instead he simply extended his hand for John to shake.

"John," he said in his best fatherly voice. "Good to meet you."

"Good to meet you too, sir," the young man replied, sounding just as tentative as Eliza had. Michael smiled at him, feeling a little relieved. John was polite and humble, not the least bit self-absorbed. All of a sudden he could see why Eliza liked him.

"Call me Michael, please," he said as he took Eliza's hand and led them into the kitchen, where Carolina was busy making lunch.

"I didn't hear you come in!" she said when she saw her daughter, then rushed over to hug and kiss her like they hadn't seen one another in years.

"And you must be John," Carolina said when she finally pulled away from her daughter. Her eyes fell on the young man, and for a moment she just stood there and admired him. Something seemed so familiar about him. The way he looked, the way he smiled...Carolina felt like she had seen it all before.

Impossible, she told herself as she leaned in to give him a hug as well, but the embrace only made this sense she had stronger.

"You're not from Seattle, right?" she asked him, remembering Eliza had mentioned something about Georgia.

"No, ma'am," John replied. "Never been here in my life." He looked at Eliza, who smiled and nodded as if reassuring him he was doing fine.

"Well. Welcome to our city, then," Carolina said with a smile, trying to push those unnerving thoughts to the back of her mind. "Have a seat and I'll get you something to drink."

While their lunch simmered, Carolina and Michael sat around the kitchen table with Eliza and John, getting to know this new addition to their daughter's life. He talked about school, and how he had met Eliza; he told them about Savannah and what it had been like growing up there. Both

Michael and Carolina were impressed; he seemed like a good man, very grounded and obviously in love with their daughter. By the time lunch was served, they all felt like old, comfortable friends.

After a delicious meal—made all the better by good company and great conversation—Eliza went to the kitchen to help her mother get dessert, leaving Michael and John by themselves. The two men looked at one another, then looked away, and in a moment they were both laughing at the awkwardness they felt.

"Well," Michael said. "Are you enjoying your visit so far?"

John smiled, obviously relieved by Michael's easygoing nature. "I am," he replied. "I love your house. And it's really great to finally meet you after hearing Eliza speak so much about you."

"Oh, really?" Michael said. "Well, I hope she's saying good things."

"Nothing but the best," John said quickly. "She thinks the world of you and her mother. She's always talking about how you two are made for each other, you're soul mates, and how she hopes to be like you someday."

"Oh, really?" Michael said again, looking down at his lap, feeling a little bit embarrassed. He knew his daughter loved him, and that she admired the relationship he had with Carolina. But to hear someone else say it—especially this stranger—it felt odd to him. And yet at the same time, somehow, it also felt so right.

"Well, she's correct; we are made for each other. We are soul mates," he said, looking back up at John. "Eliza's mother and I have been through a lot together. You believe in fate, John?"

"I do," he said, his reply once again instantaneous. "I think that's how Eliza and I got together in the first place."

Michael, who had been raising his glass to take a drink, lowered it again to the table. He just looked at John for a moment. "You think fate brought you together?" he asked.

"Yes, I do, sir. I mean, there has to be a reason why we both ended up at the same school, right? And how we met—why else would we be at that same place at the same time? There had to be some larger force at play. It's just too perfect to be a coincidence. It can't be random chance that I would go all the way across the country and meet the love of my life."

Michael swallowed hard and put on a stern face, trying once again to play the concerned father. "So you're in love with Eliza?"

John sat up straight in his chair, his face betraying the nervousness he felt. Perhaps he hadn't meant to say that—especially not to Michael. But as Michael himself knew, when you experience something wonderful like that, it's so hard to keep it to yourself.

"Uh, well, yes, I do," John said. "As a matter of fact..." He stopped and cleared his throat, as if gathering his thoughts. He then took a deep breath and looked Michael in the eyes. "In fact I think your daughter is the one for me." He seemed to be gaining confidence with every word he said. Michael didn't reply; he was enjoying watching the young man's progression into fearlessness.

Love will do that to you too, he thought, smiling a little as John continued to speak to him.

"I know we're still young, Eliza and I, but we know what we feel. And with something like this, you just know when it's right. Eliza is my soul mate—I'm sure of that, though I can't say how I know it. There's just something about her I can't live without, something I feel like I've been looking for, I'd say, longer than I've been alive. Do you know what I mean?"

Michael smiled at him and leaned back in his chair. "I know exactly what you mean. I feel that way about her mother. Always have and always will." He paused for a moment, sizing John up before he spoke again. "You're really serious about this? You're really serious about Eliza?"

"Yes, sir," John replied, no wavering in his voice this time. "I've never been more serious about anything in my life."

And that was all Michael needed to hear. Though he'd wanted to find some minor flaw in John, something, anything, it wasn't possible; he just couldn't find it. Of everything he knew so far, John was a good man, a smart man, a kind man. And most importantly, he was wonderful to Eliza—Michael could sense that. The fact that John regarded Eliza just as Michael and Carolina did—as his soul mate, the long-lost missing piece of his puzzle—only made him like John more.

They were young, sure. But there was no doubt they were meant to be together…forever.

Twenty-Seven

"Oh, Mom, please? It'll be so much fun!"

On the other end of the phone line, Carolina sighed. "Eliza, I just don't know. It's been years since I've been out on a boat." For a moment her mind flashed back to that afternoon—on a friend's boat for a party, Michael holding her as she gripped the railing at the stern and shuddered uncontrollably, memories of the storm rolling through her head. "You know how I feel about them."

"I know, Mom," Eliza replied, her voice more gentle and understanding. "I know how you feel. But this would mean so much to John and me."

Carolina was silent for a moment. She didn't want to disappoint her daughter, especially right now—ever since John had proposed to Eliza during spring break, she'd been on cloud nine. Carolina just couldn't burst that bubble for her.

But still...a small engagement party on a boat? And not even a party, just an afternoon out to celebrate with the four of them—Eliza, John, Michael, and Carolina. What was her daughter thinking? She knew how she and Michael felt about the water.

I almost lost my life out there, she thought, remembering how she'd felt when she woke up alone on the beach—a day she would never forget. The sun beating down on her skin, her body bruised and broken. Michael was nowhere to be seen. She'd thought she lost him. What if the same thing were to happen again?

But it couldn't—no, it just couldn't. What were the chances? It would be too much of a coincidence. Besides, that wasn't what fate had in store for her. Not anymore. That period of her life was long over, those months of endless storms over the water, in the sky, and in her heart.

At least she hoped it was.

"Okay," she told Eliza apprehensively, "I'll do it."

But a few weeks later, she had recurring doubts. It had been easy enough to agree to the date over the phone, when the actual boat ride was a thing in the future, when it was something that didn't even exist yet. She just wanted to make her daughter happy, to give her the engagement celebration she asked for. But now that she and Michael were walking hand in hand down a pier leading out to the ocean, following Eliza and John along a row of shiny, white sailboats, she wondered what she had done, if she'd made the right decision. She clutched Michael's arm, willing her feet to keep on moving her forward.

"It's okay, babe," he whispered, shifting to put his arm around her shoulders. He held her tight. "It's not going to happen again." He looked down at her and smiled. "It's just not in the cards for us. Remember? Fate brought us together, and it's never, ever going to tear us apart."

She smiled at him too but kept her thoughts silent, simply hoping that his faith in their destiny was right.

"This is it!" Eliza called to them as she and John stopped beside a boat.

"Belongs to a friend of mine here in California," John added as Carolina and Michael walked up to them. "He always said I could borrow it anytime. He's confident with my boating experience." He turned to Eliza and threw an arm around her happily. "We take it out whenever we can. We both love the water. We've had some great times out there."

Carolina smiled at them. "Don't know where you get *that* from," she said to her daughter with a smirk, amused that Eliza could find such pleasure in something that gave her such unease.

"Mom, are you sure you're okay to do this?" Eliza asked, her face a mask of concern.

Carolina reached out to hug her daughter. "If it will make you happy, sweetheart, of course I am. I'll be fine." She pulled back and put her hand on Eliza's cheek. "I want to do whatever makes you happy."

"Thanks so much, Mom," Eliza said, a hint of tears welling in her eyes. "This means so much to me." She looked at Michael, too. "Thank you both for coming out to California."

"Anything for our little girl," Michael said, reaching out to squeeze his daughter's arm. "Now, let's get out there on the water."

Everyone climbed on the boat and as John hoisted the sail, the rest made themselves comfortable. Looking around, Carolina noticed just how much this boat looked like the one they'd been on the day of the storm. A little bigger, but essentially the same.

"It's going to be fine, sweetheart," Michael whispered to her, his face bent close to hers. He looked her right in the eyes, connecting with her as he always did, drawing her out of her fear. Little by little, she tried to let go of her uncertainty.

"What a great day for sailing!" John shouted above the sound of the water shushing around the sides of the boat as they got underway. "Not a cloud in the sky!"

Carolina smiled at him, very aware of what he was trying to do: letting her know he understood her fear of the water and at the same time reassuring her this time it would be different. John smiled in return, appearing happy that his message was received.

Once out on the open water, they drifted for a while; the sea was calm, and the motion of the boat actually helped Carolina relax. As John attended to the sail, Michael and Eliza talked and laughed at the front of the boat. Carolina retired to the rear, where she found a padded bench she could stretch out on. Taking off her sunglasses and lowering her sun hat over her eyes, she even dozed off for a short time, letting the rocking and rhythm drift her to sleep.

Not much later, she awoke, and now all three of her shipmates were up by the bow. John pointed toward the distant sky, at a clutch of clouds in the distance. Eliza and Michael followed his gaze, their faces set in concentration and concern. Carolina sat up quickly, a knot forming in her stomach, her heart dropping to her feet. She whipped off her hat and looked up at the sky. It was dark now, no more glaring sun in sight.

"Michael!" she shouted as she jumped up and ran across the boat. "Michael, what's going on?"

He turned at the sound of her voice and moved toward her, meeting her in the middle beside the mast. "Carolina, what is it?" he said, taking her into his arms. It was clear she was panicked, and he did his best to calm her.

"The sun is gone!" she replied, her voice choking as sobs threatened to work their way free from her throat. "What is John pointing at? It's a storm, isn't it?"

"Now, Carolina, it's—"

"Don't lie to me, Michael," she said, backing away from him. She scanned the heavens again. Nothing but solid gray. That patch John had been pointing to, those clouds were black and growing closer by the minute. "We have to turn back now. We have to get away from it."

Michael opened his mouth to speak again, but he was cut off by a low rumble in the distance. As he watched, Carolina's eyes grew wide like saucers. The fear in her expression was unreal, like nothing he had seen before.

"Babe, listen to me," he said, moving toward her, his hands outstretched. "Hold on to me and listen. Nothing's going to—"

"John!" Carolina called. "You have to turn us around! We have to get out of here!"

On the other side of the boat, John glanced at Eliza as if asking her what he should do. Carolina moved toward them. "Eliza, tell him we have to get out of here before the storm hits."

"Carolina!" Michael said, his voice booming and strong. Suddenly he was right behind her, grabbing her by the arms and spinning her around. "Carolina, you have to listen to me. We're going to be fine. It's just a few clouds. They're going to pass. We always survive after the storm."

"But I heard thunder, Michael," she said, and her tears flowed freely now. "It's happening again. And maybe this time we won't be able to escape it."

Michael gripped her tighter, looking once again deep into her eyes. "Babe," he said, his voice low and soothing. "You trust me, don't you?"

Carolina gazed back at him, trying so hard to grab on to that electricity, the charge that connected them to one another. In her terror she was having trouble finding it, but she wanted to. She needed to. "Yes, I trust you," she told him, feeling the spark beginning to ignite.

Michael pulled her close, pressing her head against his chest. He breathed deeply, in and out, and told Carolina to do the same. She tried to; she inhaled and exhaled, a little more every time. She closed her eyes and listened for Michael's heartbeat, letting its rhythmic sound fill her senses.

"Everything will be okay," Michael whispered to her, swaying her body back and forth. He kissed the top of her head. "We will make it through this."

Carolina slipped her arms around his back and held on to him tightly, hoping against all hope that his prediction was right. Straining her ears, she listened once again for thunder in the distance. Nothing. As if it whatever storm had been there had ceased to exist.

She let out a long breath, feeling a tiny bit of relief. She rubbed her cheek against Michael's shirt as he ran his fingers through her hair. They stayed like that for some time, until Carolina no longer felt like crying, until the panic she'd felt in her chest had subsided to a dull ache. And then—

"Baby, look up," Michael said to her, putting a hand on her chin to lift her face. He turned her toward the sky. A glowing warmth covered her skin.

It was the sun. Bursting through the clouds and pushing them away. Suddenly the sky was blue, clear as if it were a beautiful summer day.

"See? I told you we'd be fine," Michael said, and Carolina turned back to him. She gazed into his eyes, and now their fire was there immediately—as it always was, always had been, and always would be. In his eyes she saw everything she needed: protection, love, safety, desire. She couldn't believe she'd doubted him.

"I'm so sorry," she said. "I should have believed you."

Michael shook his head, the most peaceful smile spreading across his lips. "Don't apologize," he said. "Just kiss me."

And so she did. As their lips touched, new memories formed in her mind, covering up the images of that other storm, the one that had happened to them so long ago. In its place were better pictures: of Michael, the love of her life, her soul mate, smiling down at her; of their happy life, full of joy and peace and family; of their beautiful daughter and the man who would do anything for her, both of them ready to start their life together. These were better thoughts, better mementos for her to carry with her.

And she would do just that, now, forever, for eternity.